AF436484

DAMAGED

NECESSARY EVILS

ONLEY JAMES

DAMAGED
A Necessary Evils Novella

TRIGGER WARNING

This book contains depictions of and discussion
of intimate partner violence.

PROLOGUE
DR. THOMAS MULVANEY

"Thank you for agreeing to meet with me, Dr. Mulvaney."

Thomas arched a brow, studying the young woman sitting in the tattered booth across from him. Saying he agreed to meet her was a stretch. Forced would be more appropriate. The coffee shop was near deserted. People didn't want to eat in a place with sallow lighting, cracked vinyl booths, and vinyl floors that sounded like velcro when you walked on them. Once the place had probably been vibrant, but now, it was a shell of its former self—the coffee shop that time forgot. The smell of stale coffee, grease, and pancakes wasn't unpleasant but did seem overwhelming.

Outside, a vicious storm raged, condensation blotting out the windows, making the outdoors seem post-apocalyptic when lightning crashed, illuminating everything on the other side of the glass. Thunder boomed ominously, rolling towards them, before dissipating again, creating this cozy pocket of anonymity around the back booth where they sat.

Thomas had thought a great deal about the kind of person

who would dare to blackmail him, but never once had he imagined it would be the girl sitting across from him. She was young, but she had a wariness about her, a cynicism etched in her steely gaze that made Thomas both curious and uneasy.

She dressed like any normal teenager—jeans and a Kiss t-shirt, a black unzipped sweatshirt with the hood pulled up, leaving just a heavy fringe of inky black bangs visible. She was pale—not fair skinned, just lacking sunlight. She had husky blue eyes and a smattering of freckles across her pierced nose. She reminded him of his youngest, Adam, though she was much older.

She seemed…not nervous, exactly. More resigned. Like she didn't like what she was doing but she had no choice. Blackmail was a tedious thing, no doubt. He'd expected his blackmailer to be some hulking ghoulish figure full of malice and rage. Thomas could have dealt with that easily. But this… This was far more unnerving. There was nothing so dangerous as somebody who had nothing to lose, and she looked like she had nothing to lose.

When she didn't continue, Thomas said, "What is it I can do for you…" He let the question linger, hoping she would fill in the blank, but she just stared at him until he asked, "Do you have a name?"

She quirked up a well manicured brow, a small smirk curving across full lips painted the color of dried blood. "Doesn't everybody?"

"Can you tell me yours?" Thomas prompted.

She thought on it for a moment. "You can call me Calliope."

Thomas tilted his head. "Because that's your name, or because you don't want to tell me your name?"

"Yes," she said, deliberately obtuse.

Thomas laced his fingers together on the scarred wooden table between them. "How can I help you, Calliope?"

The woman reached into her pocket and pulled a picture free, slapping it on the counter between the two of them. It was a picture of a young boy. He was clearly related to her. He had her same blue eyes and freckles, though his hair was a warm brown, not inky black. He might have been five or six.

Thomas frowned, picking up the photo and examining it closely. There was something…reptilian in his gaze, a calculating shrewdness that made the hair on Thomas's arms stand up. He was all too familiar with that look. "Is this your brother?"

She shook her head. "My son."

"Your…son?" Thomas echoed, unable to hide his surprise.

She nodded, picking up the wrapper that had once contained the straw now sitting in her untouched Diet Coke. "I had him when I was sixteen. His name is Dimitri. I need your help."

Thomas watched as she proceeded to tie the straw wrapper into knots until it came apart between her fingers. She frowned, disappointed, before tossing it to the side.

Thomas struggled to understand the point of this meeting. Was she trying to blackmail him for money? If so, why show him the picture of her son? To garner sympathy?

None of this made sense. Thomas had more money than he could spend in ten lifetimes. If all she needed was financial help, he'd be willing to give her whatever she needed to get by. "If you're looking for money—"

"I'm not," Calliope snapped, the venom in her tone evaporating almost immediately. "I'm not," she said again, softer. "My son—" She swallowed. "My son is like your sons."

"Like mine?" Thomas parroted cautiously, even though it was clear what she meant.

Calliope met his gaze. "My son is a psychopath."

Thomas felt a shock of adrenaline rocket through him. Shit. "I don't know what you're implying—"

Calliope held up her hand. "Don't bother pretending I'm crazy. I've hacked your system, read your files, your case studies, all of your sons' dossiers. I've seen it all."

Thomas's mind reeled. It wasn't possible. His research files were hidden behind software that would make the CIA's look primitive. "Do you...work for the government?"

That didn't make any sense. She didn't look old enough to drink.

She stared at him sullenly. "Do you?"

Finally, he shook his head. "No. I don't."

Not exactly. There were several high-ranking officials among all branches of the government who followed his research. It took a great deal of time and money to do what he did, but more than that, it took connections. Connections that would disavow any knowledge of him and his experiment if those not in the know were to find out.

Her shoulders slumped. "Me neither."

She gazed out the foggy window for a long moment before lifting a finger to trace a drop of water as it created a path through the haze.

"May I ask how you found me?" Thomas asked, taking a sip of his lukewarm coffee.

She was quiet for a long moment, stirring the carbonation out of her soda. "When I realized my son wasn't…normal, I started researching. The usual stuff at first, but the more I tried to find help for my son, the clearer it became that there was nobody with any kind of definitive answers on my problem."

She wasn't wrong. "How did that lead to me?"

Calliope's gaze met his. "It didn't. At first. Then I found Dr. Molly Shepherd. Her research on sociopaths was groundbreaking but purely theoretical. So, I hacked her files and found…you."

Molly Shepherd. She was the reason his whole project existed, the reason for the entire experiment. The reason he was raising seven psychopathic sons to become killers. He supposed the correct term would be vigilantes. Dr. Shepherd didn't approve of his methods, but she kept track of his research just the same. They all did.

"Me?" Thomas asked.

"Are we going to do this the whole time?" she asked. "I know who you are. I know what you're doing. I know what your sons are. I know who they are and where to find them. I know your bank account info, your social security number. I know the color of the last pair of underwear you bought. *I know.* Please, stop wasting our time."

Before Thomas could question the validity of her statements, she slid a piece of paper towards him. On it was his social security number. Was that proof she had what she said she did? No. But why would he doubt her when she clearly knew more than anybody else?

"How can I help you, Calliope? If you're looking for somebody to take your son, that's not how I work."

Calliope looked at him with wide eyes. "What? No. I-I'm not trying to give you my son. I'm asking for help. I need to know how to take care of him. How to keep him from growing up to be a monster."

That was the thing about psychopathy. There was no real way to keep them from becoming whoever they would be. Not all psychopaths were murderers. In fact, most weren't. But that didn't mean they weren't dangerous, that they were good people. Psychopaths were born weapons. Thomas just made sure those weapons were pointed at those deserving of whatever fate they received.

But he couldn't tell any of that to her.

Thomas leaned in. "We don't diagnose psychopathy in children."

She thrust her jaw forward, crossing her arms over her chest. "Yet, somehow, you have a household full of child psychopaths."

Okay, she wasn't wrong. But he hadn't specifically set out looking for psychopaths, just children who were showing psychopathic tendencies. "Have you had him evaluated?"

Calliope hesitated before nodding. "Yes. Like you said, they don't diagnose children, but I know they see it. Even if they won't say it. The last therapist he had…whatever he said to her, she refused to see him again after that. Do you know how fucked up you have to be to scare off a child therapist in our neighborhood?"

Thomas didn't. He didn't even know where her neighborhood might be. But he believed her. She looked like somebody who wasn't used to feeling helpless. Her frustration was evident in the draw of her mouth, the exhaustion behind her eyes.

"Can you give me specifics?"

She shook her head in a sort of helpless motion. "He has no empathy…for anybody. No impulse control. His rage is instantaneous. When other kids piss him off, he reacts fast and with violence. A little boy stole his truck on the playground, and Dimitri shoved him off the jungle gym. The boy broke his arm in two places. I watched my son pick up his truck and begin playing again like there wasn't a boy screaming in agony a foot to his right."

Thomas understood the woman's concern, but the boy was young. Kids compartmentalized. They were often selfish and possessive of toys. "Anything else?"

She closed her eyes and took a deep breath. "He set our neighbor's bed on fire."

Thomas's eyes went wide. Arson. That was a bad sign. "Tell me what happened."

"There's a little boy next door. Small. Shy. Really quiet. Dimitri has developed a kind of fixation on him. He's very protective. The boy's always got bruises on him. After what happened on the playground, I thought maybe Dimitri was hurting him."

Thomas's tone was grim. "Was he?"

"It was the boy's father. Dimitri stayed over there for a sleepover after a soccer match. It was him and a few other boys. While the other boys were sleeping, he poured nail polish remover on the parents' bed and set it on fire. They were still in it." She stabbed her straw into the ice in her soda. "How does a five-year-old even know how to do that?" she said, giving a humorless laugh.

"And the police didn't step in?" Thomas asked.

"The man didn't press charges because he only had a small burn on his leg, and he obviously didn't want the cops to get a look at the bruises on his son. I lucked out, I guess."

Thomas sighed. "The arson is concerning, but it's encouraging that he did it in retaliation for injuries inflicted on another person. Any abuse of animals? Bed wetting?"

Calliope just shook her head again, taking a sip of her Diet Coke before wrinkling her nose. "He's not a bad kid. He just sometimes does bad things. But there's just—" She gave a huge sigh. "There's just something missing in him. I don't want to lock him away. I couldn't even if I wanted to. There's no place to put him. They don't want to help a child before they do something violent. Only after."

"What specifically are you asking of me, Calliope?"

She looked him directly in the eye. "Help me teach my son how to be a person, a productive member of society. I can't pay you, but I have skills that might be beneficial to you, considering what you do."

What he did... To the rest of the world, he was just

another one-percenter with a charitable foundation used as some kind of tax write-off. They were a little easier on him because of his tragic past and the fact that he'd adopted seven children, but there were whispers about that as well. He shook the thoughts away.

"Skills?" he asked.

"I'm a hacker. A good one. Hell, a great one. Possibly even the greatest ever. I've never met a system I couldn't hack. I have a day job, but it's a solitary job. Nobody watches me. I can be at your beck and call. Just help me. Please."

Calliope clearly wasn't somebody accustomed to asking for help. She looked like she'd rather have a root canal than beg a rich stranger to save her son, but there she was, doing it anyway.

Thomas could use somebody like her. There was no doubt about that, but how did he teach somebody to curb impulses in their child that he blatantly encouraged in his own? "And if I can't help you?"

Calliope stared at him with dull eyes. "Then, at some point, my son is going to snap and kill somebody and the blood will be on both our hands."

ONE
DIMITRI

It was impolite to stare. It was something Dimitri's mother had drilled into his head from the time he was little. Don't stare. Don't obsess. Don't let people see who—no, not who, but what—you really are. Normal people didn't like that, didn't find his stalkerish tendencies romantic or flattering.

The thing was, Dimitri had never obsessed over anybody but Arlo, had seen nobody but Arlo from the moment he'd dragged his mat next to Dimitri's in Mrs. Faison's preschool class and confessed he was afraid of the dark. Dimitri had assured him that he was afraid of nothing and that had reassured Arlo enough to fall asleep.

Arlo didn't remember that, and he didn't remember Dimitri. After Dimitri had set Arlo's parents' bed on fire, his mother had moved them away, away from prying eyes and away from Arlo. But Dimitri had found his way back. The moment he'd gotten his license, he'd learned where Arlo was, what he was doing, and had found a way to make their paths meet again.

Not that Arlo knew any of that. As far as he knew, he and Dimitri were just friends due to circumstance. They both needed money, so they both worked at the campus coffee shop, which was where Dimitri now sat, taking his thirty minute break with a group of people he called friends. Well, who called him a friend. Truthfully, he wouldn't care if a hole opened up and swallowed them up right in the middle of Hallowed Grounds.

"You're going, right, Dimi?"

Perfectly manicured fingers appeared, snapping an inch from his face. Dimitri dragged his gaze from the boy behind the counter to stare blankly at the blonde-haired girl before him. "What?"

Mandy rolled her eyes. "You never listen to me."

"To be fair, you never stop talking," Jason said. "It's hard to keep up."

Mandy gave him the finger and a pissy look, which only made Jason more bold. Mandy liked the attention, though. She liked any and all attention. But Jason was right, she never stopped talking. And never about anything that interested Dimitri. She talked about frat parties, and football games, and, well, Dimi. She'd been trying to get with him since the start of senior year, and not even his sexual orientation seemed to stop her constant attempts to trick him into a date.

But Dimitri only had eyes for Arlo. Sweet, soft, dangerously pretty Arlo. As if he could hear his thoughts, the boy looked up from behind the counter and gave him a timid smile. It didn't meet his eyes. Arlo hadn't given him a genuine smile since that piece of shit, Holden, had shown up in his life.

"I can't. I have to work," Dimitri said. "I'm closing tonight. Remember?"

Mandy pouted, her bottom lip pooching out in a look that wasn't nearly as cute as she thought it was. "Can't you get somebody to cover for you? Like that kid with all the acne."

The kid in question was Remi, and he would have laughed if he'd heard Mandy's assessment of his looks. Remi's skin wasn't clear but that didn't stop the girls from throwing themselves at him. He was smart, funny, and his family was filthy rich. And, somehow, he was still a nice guy.

But no, Dimitri couldn't ask Remi to cover for him because Remi was already scheduled to close with Arlo. Dimitri would be off in twenty minutes. But he wasn't about to tell Mandy that. She was like a dog with a bone. She wouldn't let it go until she either dragged him to the party or he lost his shit and told her to get lost. Neither of those things were particularly appealing to him.

"I'll ask," Dimitri lied.

"Yay," Mandy said, bouncing on the balls of her feet and clapping her hands like she was about to break out in a cheer. Jason rolled his eyes, returning his gaze to his laptop. He'd been pretending to study since they'd sat down, but really, he was keeping an eye on Mandy. Jason really liked Mandy.

Dimitri made a production out of pulling his phone free and typing out a text to Remi, just not the one Mandy expected. **Can I take your shift tonight?**

The reply was instantaneous. **Shit, pretty boy. You can**

take all my shifts.

Dimitri did his best to hide his smirk. **I just need this one. Thanks. Oh, and if anybody asks, I was always scheduled to work this shift. Cool?**

The eyeball emoji popped up, then, **Anybody? Would anybody be stalker Barbie?**

Dimitri's only response was a thumbs up. With that settled, he slipped his phone back into the pocket of his apron and shrugged. "He said there's no way. It's his mom's birthday."

Mandy scrunched up her face. "I thought his mom was dead?"

Was she? What the fuck did he know? "Maybe he meant existentially. We're all a little dead inside, right? Maybe some other time."

Jason smirked behind Mandy, knowing full well that Dimitri was jumping through hoops trying to disentangle himself from her.

"You say that every time," she said, voice sullen.

And yet, you just keep asking. "I gotta get back to work." Mandy frowned, looking around the deserted shop, but he didn't give an explanation, just some semblance of a smile that faded as soon as he turned away from her. He heard the door open and close, signaling they'd left, but he didn't look back.

He entered the back area using the side door in the hallway. Arlo was cleaning the steam valve with a white cloth, his up and down movement unintentionally suggestive. Dimitri would give up almost anything to feel Arlo's hand wrap around him that way.

Arlo dropped the rag, giving Dimitri a lopsided smile. "Did you just lie to get out of a party?"

Dimitri returned his smile. "I didn't lie. I took Remi's shift for him."

Arlo narrowed his eyes. "When?"

Dimitri grinned. "Just now."

Arlo's responding grin was a gut punch, stealing his breath. Mandy described Arlo as a pretty twink, but he wasn't just pretty, he was perfect. He had golden skin and golden blonde hair that he wore swept back off his face like some actor in a vintage movie. Remi said he looked like James Dean. Dimitri could see the resemblance but Arlo was just sweeter, softer, innocent. He had this perfectly symmetrical face with high cheekbones that looked like they'd been sculpted by the gods.

And then there were his lips. Full and always cherry red, like he'd been chewing at them. Dimitri often thought of those lips when he was alone at night. Normally, they were glossy from chapstick or from Arlo's tongue sweeping along his lower lip several times a day. Today, those lips were swollen, the bottom one split and red with dried blood. A purple bruise marred the left side of his mouth.

Arlo always had bruises. He made excuses. He walked into the wall, fell down the stairs, bumped into an open cabinet door. *Just clumsy. I'm always daydreaming.* It was a lie. It was always a lie. They both knew it. But something in Arlo's eyes always begged Dimitri not to say it, not to say the thing out loud that would make it real.

Dimitri kept quiet. The last time he'd interceded on Arlo's behalf, he'd lost sixteen years with him. Maybe it was selfish, but he didn't want to risk losing him again. But he planned. He dreamed. He fantasized about the day he'd get revenge for what Arlo had suffered.

And he did suffer. Black eyes. Finger-shaped bruises on his arms and neck. A spiral fracture that he claimed he'd gotten from slipping on ice. Dimitri knew those kinds of fractures only happened for one reason—somebody had twisted his arm behind his back hard enough to break it.

No, not somebody. Holden. Arlo's closeted, dick bag, football player boyfriend from a rival school. Holden had money, connections, and had clearly never heard the word no. Arlo, like many abused kids, had transitioned from abusive parents to abusive boyfriends without much fanfare. It would almost break Dimitri's heart…if he'd had one.

Still, the bruise on his face was new. It hadn't been there last night when they'd closed. He gravitated closer until he was directly behind Arlo, who gasped when he spun around and saw Dimitri directly behind him, trapping him against the counter.

Dimitri reached out and caught Arlo's chin between his thumb and forefinger, watching as Arlo's honey brown eyes went wide, a small gasp leaving his lips. Dimitri wanted to swallow that sound, wanted to feel his pulse flutter beneath his fingers, wanted to hear Arlo gasp his name.

Instead, he dragged the pad of his thumb across the cut on Arlo's lip, his temper flaring when Arlo winced.

"What happened?" Dimitri murmured. "Did he do this

to you?"

Before Arlo could answer or give him some lame excuse, the bell over the coffee shop door swung open. Arlo instantly ducked from under Dimitri's arm. "Thanks for visiting Hallowed Grounds…" His voice trailed off.

Dimitri turned to see Holden standing there, his expression mutinous as he looked back and forth between the two of them. "I need to talk to you. Now."

Holden was two inches shorter than Dimitri's six foot two, but he was a walking brick wall of bulging muscles and testosterone. The idea of somebody that big throwing around Arlo sent a shock of adrenaline firing through him. Some caveman part of Dimitri pictured slamming Holden's face into the counter until his teeth shattered and blood spewed from his caved-in face. Nobody touched what belonged to Dimitri.

But Arlo didn't belong to him. Not really. Not in any way that would matter. Dimitri didn't want to be another thing that happened to Arlo, another destructive force tearing away the pieces that were left.

Arlo trembled visibly. "I'm working."

"It will only take a minute," Holden said between clenched teeth.

Arlo gave a small shake of his head. "I said everything I had to say last night."

Holden's nostrils flared, and he took a step towards Arlo, who instinctively took a step back. "Don't be like this."

Arlo's jaw thrust forward, and he crossed his arms over his chest. "Like what? Somebody who has boundaries?

Somebody who won't let you keep using them as a punching bag because you can't handle the fact that you're gay?"

Holden snarled, lunging towards Arlo, who stumbled back, even though there was three feet of mahogany between them. "You shut your fucking mouth, you little fucking who—"

"I would highly encourage you not to finish that statement," Dimitri said, allowing all humanity to leech from his voice.

Holden's gaze tore from Arlo to glare at Dimitri, as if only noticing him there for the first time. "Is this him? Dimitri, is it?" Had Arlo mentioned him? "Is this the reason you've been so fucking irrational the last couple of days? Because you're fucking your co-worker?" Holden snapped.

Dimitri tried to process Holden's words. He thought Arlo was fucking him? Why? How? If Dimitri ever managed to make Arlo his, Holden wouldn't have stood a chance. Dimitri would have already ripped out his vocal cords and showed them to him.

"Irrational? How am I irrational? Because I told you we were done?" Arlo asked, his voice rising higher.

Holden sneered. "You're always so emotional. Can we please go somewhere so you can calm down and we can talk?"

Arlo's gaze slid to Dimitri, who gave an almost nonexistent shake of his head. Under no circumstances was he going to allow Arlo to leave with him, and he didn't care if that made him seem like some kind of caveman.

Arlo squared his shoulders. "I'm working. Besides, I said everything I had to say on the phone last night. We're over. Done. I don't know how much clearer I can make it without getting the police involved."

In an instant, Holden's rage disappeared, a calculating smile appearing in its place. "My father's a fucking federal judge. Do you think cops scare me? The chief of police came to my tenth birthday party. You're just prolonging the inevitable. I always get what I want."

Arlo swallowed audibly. "I said no. I meant no."

Holden took a deep breath and forced it out through his nose. "You can't just walk away from me. I know where you live. I know where you work. Hell, I know where your mom lives. Maybe I should tell her you've stopped taking your medications. She'd believe me, you know. She loves me, remember?"

Arlo's eyes filled with tears. "You stay away from my mother. Stay away from me."

Holden's gaze hardened. Arlo had shown weakness, and now, Holden had the upper hand. "They'll send you back to the loony bin. They'll lock you up and throw away the key. Hell, maybe your old friend, Melvin, still works there. I bet he misses your late nights together."

Arlo's face grew chalky, sweat beading on his upper lip and forehead. "Shut up," he whispered.

Holden doubled down, advancing on the counter until his hands were planted against the wood. "You don't want to fuck with me, you little bitch. I'll ruin your life."

Dimitri was moving without thought, vaulting over the counter and snatching Holden by his hair, smashing his face against the countertop, then holding a paring knife to his carotid artery. "One more fucking word and I'll *end* yours. You decide."

Holden's breathing increased, and Dimitri knew he was trying to decide if he was serious. If he would really kill him in the middle of the campus coffee shop. The answer was yes. Yes, he would. He'd kill him and go to prison and never look back.

All the fight left Holden as he seemed to realize there was no way out. Dimitri released him, and he stumbled back a few paces. "You fucked up, bro. You fucked up so bad. I'll bury you both. Just wait. I'll fuck up your whole world."

With that, he was gone. Dimitri hopped the counter a second time, cupping Arlo's face and forcing him to look at him. "Hey. Hey, you're okay." Arlo's eyes were dull and hazy, like he was locked in his own head. Dimitri let his thumbs rove over his cheekbones. "Hey, listen to me. You're good. I won't let him hurt you anymore."

Arlo took a step back, and Dimitri let his hands fall.

Arlo walked towards the double doors that led to the employee restroom before looking back over his shoulder at Dimitri. "He's right, you know. He's going to fuck up my whole world."

No, the fuck, he wasn't.

TWO

ARLO

Arlo hid in the bathroom, unable to stop the hot tears rolling down his cheeks or the sobs that racked his body. He sat in the corner, grateful he'd cleaned it just an hour before. He'd expected Holden to get violent. With him, it was almost a given. Arlo could set his watch by his outbursts. But bringing up Fountainview, bringing up that piece of shit tech who'd abused him in ways Arlo could never wash away? Somehow, that hurt worse than any physical blow.

Maybe because Holden was right. His mother would believe him over Arlo. She believed anybody with money and status and thought, in her addled brain, that if she just catered to their every whim she'd gain access to the life she always wanted, the life she blamed Arlo for taking from her. His mother thought any abuse could be endured if the apology gift had a big enough price tag.

Arlo startled at the knock on the door. "Occupied," he said, voice thick with tears.

"Arlo?"

Arlo's heart squeezed at the sound of Dimitri's voice, low and smooth and always calm. Nothing rattled Dimitri. Ever. Not even when he'd held a knife to Holden's throat… for Arlo. To protect him.

"I'll be out in a minute," he said, hating the way his voice lifted at the end in that almost feminine way that had driven his father nuts from the time Arlo was just a little boy.

There was a hesitation, then the sound of the door handle turning, then a hand jutted through a crack in the door, holding a plastic bottle. "I thought you might want some water."

The gesture only made Arlo cry harder. He clapped a hand over his mouth to hide the pathetic whimpers, then grabbed the water bottle, grateful when the door closed once more. Arlo sniffled, pressing his head back against the cold tile, taking a few sips of the frigid water. "Thanks," he said, not even sure Dimitri was still on the other side of the door.

"You're welcome."

Arlo gave a watery smile, wiping his nose with the back of his hand. Dimitri. Arlo lifted his hand, closing his eyes, allowing his own thumb to trace the pattern Dimitri's had taken just seconds before Holden had ruined everything. Arlo had thought he might kiss him. He'd looked into his eyes with such…intensity.

But that was Dimitri. Intense. He was like some brooding YA hero. Tall and muscled, chestnut hair swept away from his perfectly chiseled square jaw, and pillowy lips that Arlo dreamed of feeling on his. Not that he ever would, especially not after what had just happened in the shop.

Arlo took another swig of his drink just as Dimitri's voice came from the other side of the door. "You know, I would keep you safe…if you would just let me."

"What?" Arlo asked, breathless.

There was no answer. Dimitri must have walked away. Who said something like that and then just walked away? Dimitri. He was complex; contemplative and quiet one minute, laughing and joking with moronic frat boys the next. Jekyll and Hyde. Arlo had no way of knowing which was the real Dimitri. He clearly had no ability to gauge who people truly were on the inside.

Arlo's mother used to joke that if they'd set him loose in a room full of angels, he'd find the demon hiding in their midst. And then, he'd try to date him. She wasn't wrong. His mom said he was just attention seeking. His therapist called it a destructive pattern. A cycle of abuse. Only, instead of Arlo becoming the abuser, he just kept casting himself as the victim.

Logically, Arlo knew it was true. He knew the signs and even had a whole pamphlet with a handy-dandy checklist with the snappy BuzzFeed-like title, '**How to Tell if You're the Victim of Intimate Partner Violence.**' That was what they called it now. Intimate partner violence. Was there intimacy in that? Nothing Arlo had ever done with Holden felt intimate anymore. Maybe it never had.

Arlo hadn't loved Holden. There wasn't much to love about him. He was a closeted, entitled, one-percenter, who had been told he was a catch his whole life. Still, he'd paid attention to Arlo, complimented him, romanced him. And

Arlo knew in his gut there was a barely contained rage brewing just beneath Holden's surface. But he'd ignored it, like he always did. Why?

Because it felt familiar, normal. Besides, who else was going to want Arlo? He was pretty, too, but not in the way Dimitri was. He was big and strong and fit right in with every crowd. Arlo was too pretty, too feminine, too soft. Too mentally damaged. Too needy. Always so fucking needy.

Holden had made him forget that for a while. The beginnings were always the best. The love bombing, the courtship, the honeymoon phase. It was a roller coaster climbing to the peak, exhilarating. But, inevitably, the car tipped and then came the pain, the excuses, the gaslighting, and just when it felt like Arlo couldn't take one more second of the abuse, the love bombing started all over again. On and on and on.

He just wanted somebody to love him as he was. Was it so wrong to want just one person to look at him and see something worth loving? His therapist told him love shouldn't hurt, but it was the only kind of love he'd known.

Except for Dimitri.

Dimitri had been protecting Arlo since they were both little. They'd met when they were practically babies, back when Arlo's parents were still pretending they had the perfect suburban dream. Dimitri had blown it all up. Literally. But Arlo wasn't mad. He'd done it to protect him. Dimitri was the only person who'd ever tried to protect him.

Dimitri didn't think Arlo remembered him. When he'd met him on the first day of work, he'd seen that spark of

recognition, but then Dimitri had just held out a hand and introduced himself, so Arlo had done the same. What was he going to say? *Aren't you the kid who set my parents' bed on fire?*

Yet, in the four years they'd worked in the coffee shop, Dimitri had never once mentioned it, never once brought it up. But he was still very protective of him...just in a boring, platonic way. Arlo didn't blame him. Girls and guys constantly threw themselves at Dimitri, and though he never seemed to be interested in any of them, he definitely enjoyed the attention.

Dimitri's muffled voice came through the door once more. "Hey, I'm not trying to rush you, but it's ten 'til three."

"I'm coming," Arlo said.

The three o'clock onslaught was the worst. They would be slammed in waves until closing. He shook thoughts of Dimitri away, splashing cold water on his face and drying his hands before he returned to the front, replacing his apron and hoping his face wasn't too puffy.

Dimitri was helping a girl in a low-cut top and jean shorts that definitely didn't cover her ample ass. She stood with her hip cocked against the counter and her arms folded under her large chest. Arlo was somewhat appeased by Dimitri's seeming indifference towards the ginger-haired girl's obvious efforts. When he saw Arlo, he caught his gaze and held it before giving him a lopsided smile that Arlo felt like a caress.

After what felt like an eternity, Dimitri returned his attention to the customer, leaving Arlo standing there, adrift. He shook his head, throwing his apron back on and nailing his fake smile into place before turning around.

"I can help the next customer over here."

For the next five hours, they worked side by side in the chaos. It was a carefully choreographed dance they'd done a hundred times before, easily slipping around each other, arms touching, sides brushing, Arlo ducking under Dimitri's arm so he didn't have to slow his process.

The routine was just what Arlo needed to push thoughts of everything but work aside, and if his mind started to wander, Dimitri would pull him back with a gentle nudge, pointing him towards the throng of people in line.

As always, the coffee shop became a ghost town at nine-thirty, the students abandoning Hallowed Grounds for the Starbucks on the other side of campus. It was a much bigger storefront and was open until midnight. That suited Arlo and Dimitri just fine. They could check off their closing tasks and maybe get out of there at a reasonable time.

Dimitri deserved to get off at a reasonable time. He'd been there since they opened, only staying behind to get out of going to that party with Mandy. "You can go, you know. I can close up here. I don't mind."

Dimitri stopped cleaning, pointing his frown at Arlo. "What? No. I'm not leaving you here alone."

Arlo gave a humorless laugh. "I'm a big boy. I can take care of myself."

Dimitri didn't laugh back, didn't even so much as crack a smile. "I'm not going. It's only thirty minutes, then we can leave together."

Together… Arlo wished.

Why was Dimitri so hell-bent on protecting him? It didn't make any sense, really. What made somebody so instantly protective of another?

"Did you mean it back there, or were you just being nice?" Arlo blurted.

Dimitri arched his brow. "Mean what?"

Arlo's face flushed hot. God, he was such an idiot. "Never mind," he mumbled.

He tried to duck under Dimitri's arm like he'd done a hundred times that day, but Dimitri must have anticipated his move because he planted his hand low against the wall, ensuring Arlo couldn't escape. That left him no choice but to turn and look up at Dimitri or stay with his back to him, neither of which seemed like a great option.

"Mean what?" Dimitri murmured, his voice warm, almost teasing.

Arlo let his eyelids float closed, unable to look at him as he said, "That you'd take care of me if I let you."

He sucked in a sharp breath as fingertips caressed his cheek. He was half convinced this was some kind of sensory hallucination, that Holden had hit him and killed him and Dimitri was just some heavenly apparition gifted to him as a reward for all his pain and suffering. "I meant it. But you have to ask. I can't just step in without your permission. My mother says normal people don't do that."

Arlo vaguely remembered Dimitri's mother. She was pretty in the kind of nineties grunge aesthetic that was popular towards the end of the decade. Black hair, tattoos, pale blue eyes just like Dimitri's. Did he talk about Arlo to his mom? What did he mean by 'normal' people?

Arlo's lids fluttered open to find Dimitri examining his face, his lower lip trapped between his teeth. "What?"

"I like looking at your face," Dimitri said, his voice a rough whisper, like he was imparting a huge secret.

Arlo shook his head, bemused. "I like looking at your face, too. I always have."

"Always?" Dimitri asked, his head dipping lower until they were only inches apart.

Forever. Arlo had wanted Dimitri since before he was old enough to even know what wanting somebody like that meant. "Since the day I dragged my mat over to yours in pre-k."

Dimitri's eyes widened. "You remember that?"

Arlo scoffed, shaking his head. "I remember everything. Who forgets the boy who set your parents' bed on fire?"

Dimitri sighed. "My mom made us move after that."

Arlo leaned back against the wall. "My parents told me you'd been put in jail."

Dimitri rolled his eyes. "Please, your shithead dad wouldn't risk the cops realizing he was hurting you."

Arlo frowned, keeping his voice low only because the conversation felt so heavy. "Why'd you do it? Are you crazy? I mean, I am, too. I'm not judging. But did you know they would die if you did it?" Dimitri nodded, not even an ounce of regret in his eyes. "And you didn't care?"

Dimitri's fingers trailed from his cheek to his throat, his thumb settling over Arlo's pulse. "I cared. I wanted them to die."

Dimitri had to feel Arlo's pulse racing. Maybe that was what he was doing—judging Arlo's reaction to such a bold statement. He should have felt horror, revulsion. Dimitri was standing there telling Arlo he'd tried to murder his parents in the most gruesome way possible. But, to Arlo, it felt like somebody was handing him roses.

"Why?" Arlo knew why, but he wanted to hear him say it.

"Because they were hurting you. I promised to protect you."

Arlo shook his head. "We were five."

"Even at five I knew you were mine."

Arlo was certain the air had just been punched from his lungs. "You can't say stuff like that."

"Why?"

"Because…" Arlo floundered. "You just can't."

Dimitri frowned. "But why? Why can't we just tell the truth?"

"And what is the truth?" Arlo asked, his head swimming.

"That you belong to me. That you're mine."

Arlo slid down the wall until he was sitting on the floor of the short hallway that led to the back, his legs tucked to his chest as he attempted to process Dimitri's matter-of-fact statement. Dimitri joined him on the floor, like it was the most normal thing in the world, legs criss-crossed in front of him.

"Does that scare you?"

"It should," Arlo said. "Right? It's an insanely unhealthy thing to say. My therapist would have a field day with it. Tell me I'm falling into old patterns, changing out one abusive guy for the next."

"I would never hurt you," Dimitri said vehemently.

"Maybe not physically. But there's more than one way to hurt somebody. How long before you're controlling where I go, what I eat, how I spend my money. Who I'm friends with?"

Dimitri's eyes went wide. "I would never do that to you. I don't want to control you. I just want to keep you safe. That's all I've ever wanted."

Arlo wanted so badly to believe him. "My therapist would say you were co-dependent."

Dimitri shrugged. "My therapist says I'm a psychopath."

Arlo swallowed audibly. "What?"

"I'm a psychopath," Dimitri stated again, casually.

"What does that even mean?" Arlo managed.

"It means I lack empathy and remorse. It means I don't feel guilty about the things I do, no matter who they hurt."

Arlo blinked. "You're serious. You're…really a psychopath."

"Yeah. It's just a diagnosis like any other. There are lots of us out there. Most of us don't know it, though. My mom recognized the signs early and got me help."

"The signs? You mean when you tried to kill my parents?" Arlo said, somehow finding the whole conversation a little funny. His therapist would call it an inappropriate fear response. He called it being crazy.

Dimitri nodded. "Yeah, right after we moved."

Arlo leaned in, mesmerized when Dimitri did the same. "What do you mean when you say I'm yours? Like, you see me as a little brother or…"

Dimitri swooped down, capturing Arlo's mouth in a kiss that lingered. His whole body felt hot then cold, his hands reaching up to clench in his shirt, holding him there.

"So, not a little brother, then," Arlo said when they parted.

"No. Not as a little brother."

THREE

DIMITRI

Dimitri's heart pounded, some feral part of him wanting to drag Arlo into a closet and claim him, to mark him up like Holden had but with bites and bruises that made Arlo moan, not cry. But Arlo deserved better than that. He'd been manhandled enough by people like Holden. Dimitri wouldn't treat him like something disposable.

Dimitri gripped Arlo's hands, still clenched in his t-shirt, pulling them free and kissing the backs of them, watching his cheeks turn pink. "Let's finish up here, and then we can go back to my place. Okay? Just to talk."

Dimitri's lips twitched in an aborted smile at the look of disappointment on Arlo's face. "Just talk?"

Dimitri couldn't help but plant another kiss on his lips. "We'll see. I'm going to take out the garbage. You finish cleaning the espresso machine. Then we can both mop up and get out of here."

Arlo frowned. "I can do the garbage. You did it last night."

"No. I don't want you out there alone in the cold. Just do

the machines. I've got this."

Arlo looked like he wanted to argue, but he just took a deep breath and let it out, nodding.

Dimitri gathered the bundles of garbage from the large rubber bins around the restaurant, setting them at the back, before pushing open the heavy door and snagging the brick they used to keep it ajar. The door had been broken since Dimitri started. No matter how many times they complained, the owner, Maggie, waved them off, saying she'd take care of it the following week. They'd given up on asking.

The frigid night air robbed Dimitri of the air in his lungs. He hadn't bothered with a jacket. He wouldn't be out there long enough for it to matter. He watched the clouds form with each breath, goosebumps erupting over his skin as he reached for the bags.

He grabbed the two heaviest first, hauling them towards the dumpster and heaving them over the side where they landed with a thud. They'd cleaned out the fridges, making the enormous bags heavier than usual. It would have taken Arlo twice as long to get rid of them.

Arlo.

Dimitri's mother would tell him to leave the boy alone. She knew they worked together. She didn't like it, but she had agreed to it as a compromise as long as Dimitri left Arlo at work. She said the more he was around Arlo, the more tenuous his control was on his impulses. Dimitri didn't feel like that was true.

He did everything his mother asked of him. He laughed,

joked, went to parties—well, parties where Mandy was unlikely to attend. He did all of the things 'normal' college students did. On the surface, he was just like everybody else.

Despite what his mother might believe, he didn't have some overwhelming compulsion to kill. He wasn't up at night fantasizing about ritualistic corpse mutilation or jerking off to snuff films. He just believed that people should earn their right to share the planet with the rest of the world. People like Holden need not apply. There was nothing he could contribute to society except rape jokes and college hazing scandals. Holden wasn't a person. He was a walking caricature of a CW villain.

And now, Arlo knew it. Arlo saw what a piece of shit he was and he was going home with Dimitri instead. Warmth pooled low in his belly. Arlo had kissed him back so sweetly. Arlo had wanted more. Dimitri wanted more, too, but he was determined to take it slow. That was what normal people did. They dated, they got engaged, and then married, and then had—

Dimitri's vision split in two, his eyes somehow pointing in two different directions as his head exploded. Had he been shot? No. He hadn't heard a gunshot. He spun around, doing his best to hold himself upright, but it was almost impossible. He stumbled, the gravel shifting beneath his feet as he saw his attacker.

Fucking Holden. Holding a goddamn baseball bat. Of course, he'd hit him while his back was turned. Dimitri raised his hand, feeling the back of his head, a bit relieved when he realized his skull was still intact though sticky with blood.

He forced his shoulders back, looking his assailant in the eye. "I'd say you hit like a girl, but I know girls who could hit way harder than that."

His jab had the desired effect. Holden choked up on the bat and charged Dimitri with a primal scream. Dimitri waited until Holden cocked his arm back to take another swing, bringing his booted foot down on the side of Holden's right knee, enjoying the way he screamed and the crunch pop of his knee giving way. Dimitri watched Holden hit the ground, managing two steps before his vision tunneled to a pinpoint. He didn't feel himself fall, just knew he was on the ground, the cold gravel digging into his cheek and seeping through his t-shirt.

He wanted to move, but his brain and body seemed at odds with each other. A heavy weight fell on him, dirt and pebbles filling his mouth a split second before something sharp punctured his neck, far enough away from his carotid not to kill him but the sensation was unpleasant nonetheless. Hot blood trickled down his chilled skin.

Holden's fetid breath panted against his cheek. "How do you like it, huh? How do you like being the one pinned down with a knife to your throat?"

Dimitri doubted this was the first time Holden had done this. He loved being feared too much. But Dimitri wasn't afraid of anything, not even death.

"Just do it," Dimitri taunted. "Cut my throat. If you're waiting for me to beg for my life, you'll die disappointed."

Holden grunted, slamming Dimitri's head against the

ground, once more making him see cartoon stars. "You think you're so fucking tough. You talk so much shit. I bet you wouldn't be so tough if I went in there and dragged your little boyfriend out."

Dimitri went rigid beneath him, his nostrils flaring.

Holden's laugh was sinister. "He is your boyfriend, right? 'Cause he's definitely not mine. I've seen the way he looks at you. He's a walking heart-eye emoji. He never shuts the fuck up about you. Dimitri this, Dimitri that. I really don't fucking get it."

A million emotions warred within Dimitri at Holden's words. Arlo talked about him, couldn't shut up about him. Until tonight, he'd never imagined Arlo really thought about him much at all. But hearing that had him grinning despite his predicament.

Holden spit in his face. "Keep smiling, pretty boy. You won't be so pretty by the time I'm done with you."

The knife suddenly pierced his cheek dangerously close to his eye, then began to slowly drag down his cheek. The cut was shallow but stung like fire.

"When I'm done with you, I'm going to give him the same scar. You two can be a matching set. Maybe it will be my going away present to him." Once more, that sinister snicker that made Dimitri see red. "Well, one of them. He was always good at that. Maybe I'll fuck him one last time. Sometimes, he even cries."

There was no missing the intention in his words. Dimitri had to get him up and off him. He needed leverage, but Holden had fifty pounds on him. He shifted his weight,

but Holden countered.

"Yeah, that's it. Fight me. Give me a fighting chance at a self-defense plea. Not that my father will ever let me see the inside of a courtroom. As far as anyone will know, you were both killed in a tragic robbery gone wrong."

Killed? This idiot would be caught before sun up. Before Dimitri could retort, the back door slammed shut loud enough to startle even him. Then, the sound of sneakers shuffling over gravel filled his ears, followed by a grunt and a sound like a sledgehammer hitting a watermelon. Once. Twice. Three times.

Holden became dead weight, then disappeared entirely.

Dimitri couldn't see Arlo, but he could hear him sucking in painful breaths, a high-pitched whine leaving his lips before he said, "Oh, no. Oh, God. Holden? Holden?"

With Herculean effort, Dimitri forced himself into a sitting position, almost toppling back over, catching himself with his left arm. He looked down at Holden's lifeless form and the blood pouring from a wicked hole at the base of his skull. Arlo held the brick from the door in his hand.

"He's not moving," Arlo said, his gaze imploring Dimitri to fix it.

Dimitri scooted closer to the body, pressing his fingers to the side of his neck. There was no pulse. Arlo clung to the heavy brick, now coated in blood and tiny bits of bone. Arlo had concentrated his hits all in one spot, where Holden's spine met his head, most likely severing the spinal cord in one of his blows.

"He's dead," Dimitri said, falling back onto the ground

to look up at the stars swimming overhead. Yeah, no. That was a bad idea. He rolled onto his side and puked.

All at once, Arlo became a flurry of motion. "Oh, God. I need to call an ambulance for you. I need to call the cops. I'm going to go to jail. Holy fuck. I'm going to jail. I killed somebody. I killed somebody. Holy shit. I killed somebody."

Arlo's voice grew increasingly panicked. Dimitri managed to turn his head just in time to see Arlo pulling his phone free from his pocket. "Give me the phone," Dimitri said, voice sharp enough to cut through his frantic rambling.

Arlo's gaze snapped to him, and he looked relieved as he handed over the phone. Until Dimitri stuffed it into his own pocket. "No cops."

Arlo's hands waved in a helpless gesture. "What do you mean no cops? He's dead. You're hurt."

Dimitri shook his head. "Cops won't fix either of those things. I probably just have a mild concussion."

"Probably?" Arlo said, exasperated.

Dimitri rolled his head towards Arlo. "I mean, I don't have a CT machine in my back pocket, but yeah, probably."

"You're making jokes now?" Arlo said, exasperated.

"I'm not joking," Dimitri assured him. "Just let me think for a minute."

Thinking was a tall order, but there was no way he was letting either of them go to prison for that dumb fuck Holden. Especially with Holden's daddy being a judge. Arlo wouldn't stand a chance at a fair trial. This would all be so much easier if the world wasn't spinning on its axis.

Dimitri cleared his throat. "Okay. There are no cameras

back here, so nobody has any proof of anything."

Arlo made a strangled sound. "But there are cameras inside, and if they check them, they're going to see you holding a knife to Holden's throat five hours before he died."

Fuck. That was a good point. It could be fixed, but fixing it meant calling the one person in the world he didn't want involved. Fuck. Fuck. Fuck. He hoped Arlo appreciated the amount of shit he was about to take for him.

He pulled his phone, scrolling to the number he needed and hit the call button.

His mother's chipper voice was like an ice pick through his brain. "Hey, baby cakes. What's shaking?"

Normally, Dimitri found his mother's quirkiness hilarious, but he'd just taken a baseball bat to the head and there was a corpse a foot to his right, so he was low on humor.

"Hey, Mom. I…have a problem."

There was a long pause. "Problem?" she asked tersely. "A problem with your trig homework or you need bail money, Dimitri?"

Dimitri groaned, looking at Arlo, who was staring down at Holden's corpse like he was trying to will it back to life. "The kind of problem that requires an alibi and making part of a security tape disappear without disappearing."

"Christ on a crackerjack, Dimitri. What the fuck did you do?" she stage whispered, her heels quickly clicking over a tile floor.

He took a deep breath and let it out. "I killed somebody."

Arlo gasped at Dimitri's words, shaking his head as if to make him take it back. Dimitri wouldn't take it back. Arlo wouldn't make it behind bars, and if this went sideways, that was where one of them would be heading.

"What? Who?" she snapped.

He wanted to lie to her, but there was no way he could. He needed her help. "Arlo's dirtbag ex-boyfriend. In my defense, he was trying to kill me. It was him or me. I chose him."

Silence stretched between them like a wire pulled taut before his mother asked, "Where are you?"

Something loosened in Dimitri's chest. "Work. Around back."

"Cameras?"

"Not around back, no."

"Okay, good. Good. We can work with that."

Dimitri's apprehension returned. "Not really."

There was another pause and the sound of his mother's movements ceasing. "Why's that?"

"Because I may or may not have pulled a knife on said ex-boyfriend earlier in the day when he was threatening Arlo."

"On camera?" his mother whispered into the phone.

Dimitri sighed. "Yeah."

"Dimitri." The way she said his name dripped with disappointment.

"Sorry, Mom," he said, not really sorry at all.

"You better hope their video surveillance is on the cloud," she muttered, the sound of her walking filling his ears once more. "You're lucky I'm still at the office. I was supposed to be at a fundraiser for work."

"Which work?" Dimitri asked.

His mom had two jobs, both high-paying, neither of

them exactly legal. To casual acquaintances, she was a cyber-crimes analyst for a security company called Elite Protection Services. To those in the know, she was a black hat hacker doing all the shady things their golden boy Webster couldn't.

Her other job was less a job and more a calling. She was the Charlie to Dr. Thomas Mulvaney's psychopathic angels, helping clean up their homicidal messes. His mother was uniquely qualified to help Dimitri with this particular problem.

"I'm at Elite. I was supposed to MC the gala for cystic fibrosis," his mother said, her voice thick with the soft southern drawl she tended to put on for the outside world.

His mother was many things but, mostly, she was a chameleon. She'd gone to work for Thomas Mulvaney in exchange for help with Dimitri. After all, nobody knew psychopaths better than a man raising seven of them. When Thomas had heard his mentor's son, Jayne Shepherd, would be leaving a paramilitary group to join Elite's team, he'd sent his mother to work for the owner, Jackson Avery, to see whether his mentor had truly managed to tame her son's homicidal impulses.

It had taken longer than either Thomas or his mother had anticipated for Shepherd to arrive at Elite. In the meantime, Jackson had sent his mother undercover as the campaign manager for Senator Monty Edgeworth to ensure the man didn't harm his son. She'd almost quit over that assignment. But even after Thomas told her she no longer needed to spy, she found she didn't want to leave the Elite team. So, now, she did both.

His mother was the living embodiment of tinker, tailer, soldier, spy. A double agent. Hell, maybe even a triple agent. But, in the end, his mother only worked for herself. Nobody gave her orders. "What do we do, Mom?"

Her voice immediately softened at his tone. "You're sure he's dead?"

Dimitri nudged his corpse. "Very."

"Good. Dead is easier to fix than almost dead. Is his car there?"

Dimitri almost laughed at his mother's casual dismissal of Holden's death. Almost. Until he glimpsed Arlo, who sat chewing on his thumbnail, tears streaming down his face for the second time that day.

"Is his car here?" Dimitri asked Arlo.

Arlo's head snapped up, his gaze darting around, peering into the darkness. He pointed off to some point in the distance. "Yeah. Over there."

"You're not alone?" Calliope snapped.

"No, Mom. Arlo is here. Please, stop yelling and help us before the blood starts to coagulate. The car's here."

"Good. Do you have a tarp?"

Dimitri frowned, trying to imagine anything tarp-like in the coffee shop. "Um, no. I don't think so."

"Okay. Trash bags?"

They had huge trash bags. Industrial size. "Um, yeah. Lots of those."

"It's a bakery, right? Do you have gloves? Hair nets?"

"Yeah."

"Cover your hair and hands. Wrap the body in as many trash bags as it takes to ensure nothing is leaking. Put him in his own trunk. Be very aware of what you touch. If you have to move the seat to drive it, make sure you return it back exactly where it was. We're on the clock now, baby. I hope you're ready."

He looked at Arlo's devastated face. He had to be ready. He had to take care of Arlo.

"I'm ready."

FOUR
ARLO

Arlo sat frozen as Dimitri hit the speaker button and his mother's voice filled the chilly night air. "Okay, we need to make it look like you two are in one place and he is in another. I can spoof your GPS location from here forward, but I can't hide the fact that you were all at the same place at the same time should the cops come calling. Did anybody see him talking to Arlo? Was there anybody there to witness you threatening him, D?"

Arlo was somehow both hot and cold. Perspiration formed at his hairline and lower lip, but the gravel and dirt beneath him were icy, the frigid cold settling into his bones. Was this what going into shock felt like?

"We were alone in the restaurant," he heard Dimitri say, his words barely penetrating the fog in his head. Would they send Arlo to prison…or would he go to a mental institution like last time? He'd rather go to prison. There was no Melvin in prison. Melvin with his dirty fingernails and yellow teeth. Arlo shuddered. Yeah, he'd rather rot in prison.

"Arlo?"

Arlo jerked his head upwards, only then realizing he'd drifted away, his thoughts untethered. "What?"

"Did anybody know about the two of you?" Dimitri asked.

Right. Like Holden would tell his football player bros about his twinky little coffee shop hookup. They would have laughed him off the field. That was what Holden had said anyway.

In what world could somebody like me ever want somebody like you? We're not even close to being in the same league. Of course, you want to be seen with me. You have nothing to lose and everything to gain. I have a career to think about.

"Nobody saw us together. Nobody has ever seen us together. I was his dirty little secret," Arlo said, voice dull.

There was a slight pause, then Dimitri's mother said, "I'm sorry, sweetheart. He sounds like a real shitbag."

Her disgust loosened something in him, and he nodded in agreement. "Holden was a real shitbag."

"Well, hopefully, that means nobody will miss him."

"His family is going to miss him," Arlo swore, swallowing the sudden lump of fear in his throat. "He's rich. Rockefeller rich. And his dad is a federal judge."

Once more, there was a slight delay, and then Dimitri's mom exploded. "You've got to be kidding me. What the fuck, Dimitri? The president wasn't available to assassinate? There wasn't a royal in town you could publicly guillotine?"

Dimitri tried to interject. "Mom—"

"I've worked so hard to keep you on the right side of prison bars. Do you know how hard it is to raise a psychopath? Is this you acting out? Did I not give you enough attention?"

"No, Mom," Dimitri said, rolling his eyes, as if his mother was berating him over a report card and not the corpse between them, who was rapidly turning an alarming shade of cyan blue.

"Listen, if you're about to go all Avengers on me, we really need to talk in depth about target selection and preparation. Lesson one: you cannot kill the kid of a goddamn federal judge. Not on a whim, anyway."

"Mom… You said we're on the clock."

"Yeah, yeah," she muttered. "Fuckin' fuck, Dimitri. You're lucky I love you."

"It's my fault," Arlo blurted. "It was me. I did it."

Dimitri's head jerked up and he gave him wide eyes that screamed 'shut up' before practically yelling into the phone, "No. He's lying. He doesn't want me to get in trouble."

"That's not true!" Arlo cried, glaring at Dimitri, tears welling in his eyes.

He didn't want Dimitri suffering because of something he did. Holden had deserved what he'd gotten, but nobody would ever know that because his father would paint his son as an angel who fell victim to a boy from the wrong side of town. A boy who made up vicious rumors about his son. They'd probably say he'd tried to rob Holden or something. Would that help him when he went to prison? Would they think twice before fucking with him?

"Boys, none of this matters anymore. I'm not letting either of you go to jail for some domestic abusing fuckboy, federal judge's son or not. But we really have to move fast. We're on borrowed time, so save the blame game for your honeymoon or wedding anniversary or something. I'm going to hack into the cloud and find footage of you closing so I can clone it."

"We worked together last night," Arlo said, perking up.

Dimitri's mother made a noise. "I'm going to go back further than that. I don't want some spunky detective looking at a week's worth of footage and noting a pattern."

What was Dimitri's mother's name? Something Greek. Something magical. Persephone? Penelope? Calliope. That was it. Calliope.

What the hell did this woman do for a living that she was so calm in the face of her son committing murder?

"Our biggest problem is we can't erase the fact that his phone and GPS will already show he was at the coffee shop at least once today. Whether he left and came back or just staked the place out for a few hours I won't know until I hijack his navigation system."

Hijack his navigation system? Was she a spy? A government agent? A criminal? Given Dimitri's past, a criminal element in his family would make sense. More sense than a spy, anyway.

"Arlo."

Arlo's head snapped up as Dimitri's mother said his name. "Yes, ma'am?"

"Christ, that's cute. I can see why my son likes you. But don't call me ma'am."

"Sorry, ma—Calliope. Sorry," he said again lamely,

cheeks still burning from her calling him cute.

"Alright, my angels. Listen carefully. When the cops come—and they will—do not say you didn't know him. If Holden told anybody about Arlo, or if any of his friends had ever seen the two of you interacting, it can come back to bite you in the ass. Just say you knew each other, but it was a busy night and if he was there, you never noticed and you definitely didn't speak to each other. If they ask about a relationship, be vague. If they come back at you saying they know you two were a thing, just say you were afraid his family would find out he was gay. That's it. *Don't. Embellish.*"

Arlo sucked in a breath as Dimitri reached up and brushed his thumb over his lower lip. "What does Arlo say when they ask about his split lip?"

Calliope's voice turned ice cold. "Split lip?"

Dimitri was looking at Arlo in a way that made goosebumps erupt along his skin, and he was suddenly grateful his mother wasn't on video. "Yeah. It's pretty obvious Holden punched him in the face."

"He punched him in the face?" she echoed.

Arlo couldn't speak. Humiliation flooded his system, rendering him mute. It wasn't only the split lip. If the cops suspected him, they could get a warrant. They could ask to inspect his body for evidence of a struggle. They'd see bruises all over him. If they made him take his clothes off, they'd see it all. They'd know. They'd know everything. He blinked back tears.

He shook his head. "I can't do this. I can't do this."

Dimitri's gaze darted to his, his dark brows knitting

together. "You can."

He shook his head faster. "I can't. I'm a terrible liar."

Dimitri leaned over Holden's body to grip Arlo's chin, touching him for the second time in a minute, and—God help him—his dick took notice.

Dimitri's voice was warm and smooth and wrapped around Arlo like a blanket. "Look at me. Look right in my eyes." A shiver ran through Arlo as he realized they were inches apart. Even in the dark, Dimitri's eyes were so light they practically glowed. The heat of his gaze warmed the ice currently occupying Arlo's core.

He forced himself to focus on Dimitri's lips as he spoke, "You've been forced to lie for people who hurt you your whole life. I just need you to tell a few more so I can save you. Please?"

Arlo's heart literally skipped a beat. How did his brain think this was romantic? Maybe it was just the warmth of Dimitri's skin. Maybe it was the crush Arlo had had on Dimitri since they were playing with matchbox cars in the sandbox together.

Dimitri leaned in and brushed their lips together. "Please?" he whispered again.

If he was manipulating Arlo, he was doing a great job. He swallowed audibly, clenching his eyes shut before nodding. "Yeah, okay. I can do that," he said more confidently.

"Good boy," Calliope said.

"But what about your head?" Arlo asked, earning another wide-eyed look of exasperation from Dimitri. "What? It's a valid question. You can ask about my fat lip, but I can't talk about your possible concussion? That hardly seems fair."

"Concussion?" Calliope asked, her voice taking on an edge that made Arlo uncomfortable.

Dimitri gave an audible sigh as Arlo said, "Yeah. Holden hit Dimitri in the back of the head with a baseball bat."

"With a bat?" Calliope cried.

"I'm fine, Mom. It's not even bleeding," Dimitri lied.

Lying came so easily to Dimitri. Too easily, it seemed, because his mother said, "Dimitri Adonis Castellanos, don't you dare lie to me."

Arlo couldn't help the smile that spread across his face. "Your middle name is Adonis?"

Dimitri gave him an affronted look, which only made Arlo grin harder, especially when he said, "I didn't *choose* it."

Arlo collapsed into a fit of giggles, falling back onto the gravel beneath him, staring at the clear night sky overhead as he laughed hard enough to hold his stomach. Adonis. It was actually perfect for Dimitri. In class, a professor had once described Adonis as 'a youth of remarkable beauty' and Dimitri was. He really was.

None of this mattered. None of it. Arlo was officially losing it. The stress had broken him. Years of abuse and excuses and pain and it was Dimitri's middle name that had sent him careening over the edge into full-blown insanity. He covered his mouth with his hand, but still the laughter broke through.

"It's a family name," Calliope said with a delicate sniff, adding to Dimitri, "You should be proud of your name."

Dimitri had the barest hint of a smile on his face, that

almost-smirk that made Arlo breathless and…well, horny. When he finally pulled himself together, he sniffled, wiping at his face and pulling himself back up into a sitting position.

"I'm sorry," he finally said. "This is all just…a lot."

That was an understatement. He was Alice falling down a rabbit hole of murder and cover-ups. None of this seemed real. It was like he was watching it all from afar. Except, he was sitting with a dead body close enough for Arlo to smell the blood and see the ragged hole the brick had left in the base of his skull. A brick Arlo had held. A brick still sitting right beside him covered in God knew what. A shudder racked his body. He could feel his dinner trying to claw its way up his throat, but he forced it back down.

They didn't have time for his weak stomach.

Holden was a horrible person. He had done awful things to Arlo, had hurt him—on purpose—a million times. He'd enjoyed it. Had told Arlo he deserved it. He'd called him ugly, scrawny, unlovable, needy. So fucking needy. He'd made a game of humiliating him during sex until Arlo had just laid there, letting Holden do whatever he wanted.

"Nobody will ever want you."

But Dimitri did. Dimitri had never stopped wanting him, had tried to kill for him once, and would go to prison for him if necessary. Holden hadn't even been willing to tell the world Arlo existed.

Now, Holden didn't exist. Just his shell. Was his ghostly apparition watching the two of them plotting to get away with murder? Some mean part of Arlo hoped so.

"I'll need Arlo's phone and his ex-boyfriend's," Calliope

said.

"Can we just call him Holden?" Arlo asked quietly.

"Sure, sweetie. I'm sorry," she said, sounding like she meant it.

Dimitri pulled Arlo's phone from his pocket and pointed it at his face to unlock it. Once inside, he followed Calliope's terse instructions on how to create a mock GPS trail.

"Doesn't she need to do yours?" Arlo asked, voice dull.

"Please, my mom could take over my phone since I was ten. I promise you the software is already in there."

"He's right," Calliope chirped. "Phones are easy. Spoofing his car's GPS is going to be harder. What kind of car does this asshole drive?"

Dimitri looked at Arlo, whose brain froze for a solid thirty seconds before he remembered the sleek black sedan still in his line of sight. "A Mercedes. He drives a Mercedes," he reiterated.

There was a sound like bones cracking and then of nails flying over the keyboard as Calliope said, "Okay, I can work with that. What's Holden's last name?"

"Abernathy."

The typing stopped. "Joel Abernathy's son?"

"Yeah," Arlo answered, miserable.

"I know him," she said, a sneer in her words as she resumed typing. "Guess the shit-covered apple doesn't fall far from the shit tree."

A bemused smile formed on Arlo's face. Dimitri's mom was kind of crazy but in the best possible way. "How do you spoof a car's GPS?"

"By knowing how GPS signals work and giving it something better to latch onto. Don't you worry about that, my pretties. Mama's got that handled. I just need you boys to get him wrapped up and in his trunk. Clean up any evidence. If there's a murder weapon, wipe it down and put it in the bag with him. I'm going to send you a location. One of you takes his car to said location, the other needs to take Dimitri's and follow behind. Don't break any laws. Don't drive too slow. And, for God's sake, make sure all the headlights and taillights work before you leave."

Calliope was still talking. "I already have Dimitri's car set up to feed false data on his location. Once you park Holden's Mercedes, I need you both to go somewhere visible. Take pictures, post them, make a scene, do something memorable. If you can sneak into an event and make it look like you've been there a while, even better. Shoot me the location and I can fudge the data. Oh. If you've got a smart watch, leave it at work. Say you left it in your locker or your apron, whatever works for you. Cops are getting smarter every day."

Arlo didn't have a smart watch. Arlo could barely afford his phone. Unlike Dimitri, he didn't work at the coffee shop for spending money or experience; he worked there because it was the only way he ate or paid rent. His meager scholarship only went so far.

"So, that's it? We drop his body off and go...what? Party?" Arlo asked.

There had to be more to getting away with murder than that, right?"

"Oh, no. Sweetheart, your night is only beginning. This is just buying us some time to make sure you have an alibi while I figure out how to dispose of this fuck-wit."

Fuck-wit? "Oh," Arlo said, as if that all made perfect sense.

"Has Holden been texting you?" Calliope asked suddenly.

Arlo shook his head as if she could see him. "No. Well, he Snapchats me. He doesn't want a paper trail."

"If you've been messaging him today, keep messaging him. Do everything as you normally would."

Arlo frowned. "I broke up with him yesterday." Looking at Dimitri, he said, "He...he threatened to kill me. After this"—he pointed to his mouth—"he put a knife to my throat. The look on his face... I knew he meant it. I got away by doing what I always do. Placating him. And once I was in my car, I told him we were through. To stay away from me. I threatened to go to the cops. I lied and said I had proof of what he'd done."

"It's okay, sweetie. We're going to get through this. As a family," Calliope said, sounding so much like a mom—well, not his mom, but a mom. A good mom. A real mom—that he almost started crying again.

"Okay, don't forget to finish closing up and lock the doors. Stick to your routine. Don't forget to text me your location when you decide where your alibi spot will be. Make sure you shower and change any bloody clothes and stuff them in the bag with the body before you go have fun."

Fun. Would this be fun?

"Got it," Dimitri assured her.

"Okay, good. I love you."

"Love you, too, Mom," Dimitri said, like he'd done it a thousand times before.

Arlo couldn't remember the last time he'd heard those words from anybody. Ever.

There was a beep as Dimitri disconnected the call, and then warm hands were burning through the skin of his cheeks. "Hey. It's going to be alright. We're going to be alright. I promise."

Arlo looked at him. "I want to believe you. But, statistically, the numbers don't add up."

"What?"

"Every time I've told myself in the past that things would be alright, I was right exactly zero percent of the time."

Dimitri's mouth slanted over his, the soft slide of his tongue parting Arlo's lips in a kiss that made his toes curl.

When he pulled back, Dimitri said, "Things are different this time."

"Why is that?" Arlo asked, pulse jumping and cock now pressing against his zipper from too many kisses that led nowhere.

"Because now, you have me."

FIVE

DIMITRI

The address provided by his mother led to a warehouse in a rundown part of town, close to the port but far enough away that it was near deserted this time of night. A few people loitered outside of an all-night grocer and a couple stood outside of a sleazy bar with a blinking neon sign, but other than that, it was the normal transient community, pushing carts and bicycles piled with their belongings. None of them looked too long at the sleek Mercedes as Dimitri drove by. Nice cars in this neighborhood meant one of two things—somebody was profiting off of criminal activity or somebody was partaking in it. Nobody wanted to be a witness either way.

Arlo followed Dimitri in his less flashy Toyota Celica. Dimitri kept eyes on him in the rearview mirror, half afraid he would look back and find him missing just when he finally made him his. Dimitri's dick throbbed as he thought of the way Arlo would look at him, eyes wide, lips parted, pink tongue constantly darting out to wet his full lower lip nervously. Dimitri now knew what that tongue felt like against his, how breathy Arlo got when he was being kissed thoroughly. His mother told him they needed to be seen in public, but all Dimitri wanted to do was find a dark, isolated place to finish what they'd started inside the coffee shop only a couple of hours ago.

Would Arlo let him? Dimitri wanted to strip him bare and kiss every inch of him, wanted to swallow every moan as he mapped the planes of his body. He knew they should focus on the dead body in the trunk, but Dimitri had imagined burying himself in Arlo for as long as he could remember. Arlo starred in every one of his jerk-off fantasies, and there were many.

They just needed to get through this night. If they survived until morning, maybe then he could show Arlo how much he wanted him. They just needed to dump the car, create an alibi, and, somehow, stage a crime scene. Dimitri now understood why his mother had worried about him in the past. Murder was so much work. Well, murder was simple. Getting away with it took work.

The near silent engine of the Mercedes continued to purr as Dimitri put it in park and went to the small panel on the left, punching in the code given to him by his mother. The metal door rolled upwards at a snail's pace, until Dimitri hit the gas, the roof barely clearing the door. Once inside, he stepped from the vehicle, looking back to where Arlo sat with the engine still running.

Dimitri held up a hand, letting Arlo know he should stay there. His mother had said to just leave the car and go create an alibi, and Dimitri would do that, but something about her plans threw him. She'd given her instructions with confidence, but he couldn't shake the feeling she was struggling to get him out of this.

Dimitri returned the seat to its approximate location, examining the seat for any stray hairs or fibers, before closing the door just as Arlo jogged up to stand beside him.

Dimitri gave Arlo a stern look. "I told you to stay in the car."

"I don't take orders from you," Arlo said, jutting his chin forward in an adorably stubborn look.

Dimitri rolled his eyes but couldn't stop his lips from twitching in a smile. He wanted to press Arlo up against the car door and kiss him. Fuck, he was so keyed up, he wanted to bend him and fuck him right there. There was some kind of divine retribution in that, right? Fucking Arlo on the hood of Holden's overpriced toy?

Dimitri shook the thought away, pulling the gloves and hairnet free and stuffing them in his jeans pocket.

"Rookie mistake," a deep voice said from the darkness.

The warehouse lights blazed on, temporarily blinding Dimitri. He shoved Arlo behind him, blinking until the amorphous blobs before him took on the shape of people. Many people. Dimitri was most definitely outnumbered. Had his mom set him up to be ambushed? What the fuck?

There were three men who sat on a sturdy metal table and five more lounging against various sturdy fixtures.

The one with freckles and brown hair said, "Is he trying to hide the little one behind him? That's so cute."

"Who are you?" Arlo asked over Dimitri's shoulder.

One of the men grinned at Arlo. "Us? We're the A-Team. Who are you?"

Dimitri knew who they were. He knew them by name. It honestly surprised him that Arlo didn't. These men weren't exactly the Kardashians, but they made the papers almost as frequently.

Dimitri looked over all of them. The hot dark-haired one with the pale blue eyes was Adam. The baby. The former model. The brown-haired boy beside him was his boyfriend, Noah. The red-head was Atticus. A doctor. The man who stood beside him was his husband, Jericho. The twins were there, too. Asa and Avi. His mother called them the murder twins.

But it was the last man who caught and kept Dimitri's attention. August. At first glance, he looked like nothing special. The nerdy professor that the outside world thought him to be, but Dimitri knew he was the most dangerous one of all. The one who enjoyed torture, who enjoyed opening people up to see how they worked. Yet, his husband, Lucas, stood beside him, looking up at him with puppy eyes.

"Don't lie either," August warned, studying him like he was a slide under a microscope.

"I'm Dimitri." Dimitri looked at each of them. "And you're the Mulvaneys."

"And how did you and your friend come to be standing in our warehouse, Dimitri?" August continued, pacing closer.

Dimitri frowned, unsure of whether he was being tested or not. "I was told to come here by Calliope."

"And you're Calliope's…?" Atticus asked, trailing off, as if expecting Dimitri to finish the sentence.

"Son," Dimitri supplied carefully.

There was an excited whoop from Noah and Lucas and a groan from the twins.

"I told you she had a kid. Pay up, assholes," Lucas crowed.

"You said she had a kid, but you were speculating. There's no way your psychic powers work via telephone," one twin said, slapping cash into Lucas's hand.

"There's an entire network of telephone psychics who say otherwise," Noah said, tone superior. "You should know by now to never doubt Lucas's powers."

Dimitri watched them all with interest. They were all like him—psychopaths—yet, they seemed so normal, like a family. They didn't look like people who spent their nights hunting, but they did. They were killers, vigilantes, according to his mother.

But, now, so was Arlo.

"Did my mom ask you to be here?" Dimitri asked. "Are you supposed to help us?"

"Calliope specifically asked us *not* to be here," Atticus said, looking around at the others like a disappointed parent.

"Yet, you came, too, Freckles," Jericho reminded him. "It was just too good an opportunity to waste."

Dimitri couldn't imagine anybody calling the stocky ginger man Freckles, but it went practically unnoticed by the others.

Arlo stepped from behind Dimitri, taking two steps past him before Dimitri pulled him back against him, his arm an iron bar across Arlo's narrow waist. "Stay with me," he murmured against his ear.

"That's so cute," Noah said again.

Adam rolled his eyes, looking sulky at his boyfriend's assessment. Dimitri wasn't sure what they should do now. Call his mother? Try to reason with these men? It wasn't like they were going to call the cops on them. Were they?

"Who's in the trunk?" August asked.

"What?"

"Who did you kill?" the man said, enunciating this time just in case Dimitri was stupid instead of hard of hearing.

"My dickbag ex-boyfriend," Arlo supplied, his tone daring anybody to say he wasn't justified in doing so.

Dimitri stiffened as one twin approached. He didn't know who was who. When he was inches away from Arlo, he looked down at him, lifting a hand as though he might touch his face. Dimitri made a sound that was almost a growl of warning.

The man grinned, holding his hands up in an 'I surrender' pose, a look of mock innocence on his face as he backed up a few paces.

"Why are you here if my mom didn't want you here?" Dimitri managed, holding Arlo a little tighter.

It was Adam who spoke up. "Because, for as long as we can remember, your mom has been the voice of reason. She's saved our asses a thousand times, yet we've never seen her, touched her, shared a meal. We don't know her real name. We didn't even know she had a kid—"

"I did," Lucas interrupted with a little wave of his hand.

"—until today," Adam finished, glaring at Lucas.

It surprised Dimitri to hear that his mother had never spoken of him. It didn't hurt his feelings. He wasn't sure he had those. But she was always gushing about the Mulvaneys. He'd just imagined that she also talked of her life to them and Dimitri was her life. They were all each other had.

Yet, they thought her name was some kind of code name. While his mom's work revolved around clandestine meetings and criminal activity, she was a pretty straight shooter, never one to mince words, even if she tempered those words with wit and sarcasm.

Dimitri looked forward to his mother's sharp tongue. It meant she was okay. She'd spent his early years in a constant state of stress and panic…because of him. The strain of raising a psychopath on her own had all but broken her. Until she met Thomas Mulvaney.

The psychopath whisperer. That was what Calliope had called him. Now, it was what she called Adam's fiancé, Noah, who looked so innocent. The three Mulvaneys who'd found love had found it with people who were—for lack of a better word—normal.

Did that mean he could find happiness with Arlo? Only if he got him out of this mess. He wasn't sure what was happening right now. Was this some sort of posturing? Were they just truly curious about his mother?

Dimitri tilted his head to the side, letting all emotion and life drain from his face. "Are we going to have a problem?"

The twins' nostrils flared, both of them grinning in unison. But it was August who spoke, his tone soothing, like he wanted to put Dimitri at ease. "Easy, kid. We just want to help."

"How could you help me?" Dimitri asked.

"Don't you mean him?" Noah countered.

Dimitri's gaze darted to Noah. "What?"

"Yeah, your mom definitely knows you're covering for him. She didn't say who you were, but she definitely told us what happened, and she doesn't believe your story for a second."

"Why's that?" Dimitri asked, his heart thudding heavily against his ribs.

Jericho shrugged. "She said if you were going to kill him, there wouldn't have been enough left to bury. Seems your weapon of choice is fire. We thought, at first, maybe she was working for another company—" *She is.* "—but now that we know you're her son, this all makes so much more sense."

"Does it?" Arlo asked, sounding bewildered.

August looked at him. "Oh, most definitely. You lucked out, kid. Seems his mother will protect you, and that means *we* will protect you, too. So, it seems you've chosen your new boyfriend wisely, though whether he's a—what did you call the other one?"

"A dickbag," Noah supplied helpfully.

August nodded, continuing his thought. "Yes. Whether he's a *dickbag* remains to be seen."

Boyfriend. It seemed like such a meager word to describe the chemical that fired in his brain whenever Arlo was anywhere near. It felt cosmic. Animalistic. Thoughts of Arlo consumed him. But Arlo didn't know any of that. After tonight, Dimitri would show him. He'd show him every chance he got.

"I have to ask. Did the dickbag do that to your face?" Atticus asked.

"He did. That's why he's currently leaking brain matter into a garbage bag in the trunk," Dimitri answered, wrapping a protective arm around Arlo.

"What did you use?" a twin asked, voice almost excited. "A gun? A knife?"

"A brick," Arlo said, his voice barely audible.

The twin made a face. "A brick, huh? Weapon of convenience, I'm assuming?"

Arlo stiffened against him. "He had a knife to Dimitri's throat."

The other twin sneered in Dimitri's direction. "You let him get the jump on you with a knife?"

"He hit him in the back of the head with a baseball bat," Arlo said indignantly.

Dimitri placed his lips against his ear. "Easy. They're just trying to get a rise out of us."

Atticus stepped forward. "He hit you in the head? Are you okay?"

Dimitri scoffed at the man. "No, I'm not okay. I got hit in the head with a baseball bat. I have a wicked headache, and every five to ten minutes I feel like I'm on a tilt-a-whirl."

The ginger-haired man frowned. "You need a CT scan. You could have a brain bleed."

"I told you," Arlo said, tone accusatory.

Dimitri rolled his eyes. "If I did, wouldn't I be a vegetable by now?"

"Not exactly, no. You, at the very least, have a concussion."

"It doesn't matter. My mother says we're on the clock. She told me to stash the corpse here and go be seen in public to establish an alibi. Instead, I'm here playing twenty questions with you people. We still have to go home and shower, find clothes. We've probably already fucked up wasting this much time."

"You can shower here," Noah said. "We have a shower in the back for just this reason. We have clothes, too. Arlo's a little shorter than me, but he'd probably fit in Felix's clothes?" Noah looked to Jericho for confirmation. The man nodded.

"Dimitri could probably wear something of Adam's."

"My clothes are couture and very expensive," Adam said, glaring at his boyfriend.

"Shut up. The shower is in the corner. I'll leave the clothes outside the door. There's only one shower, so you might have to share. If you hand us your dirty clothes, we can get rid of them. It's the least we can do."

The mention of showering with Arlo had an immediate biological effect on Dimitri, one that pressed directly against Arlo's lower back. Dimitri loosened his grip, but Arlo didn't move away. He pressed closer. He knew just what he was doing to Dimitri, the little tease.

"Yeah, okay. We can do that," Dimitri said before tacking on a begrudging, "Thanks."

SIX
ARLO

Arlo had thought of nothing more than getting naked with Dimitri for the better part of four years and had often fantasized about him when he was having to fake his way through sex. But he'd never imagined murder being the catalyst for their first sexual encounter, and he'd never prepared himself for the thought of Dimitri stripping him naked in a shoebox-size shower room in the back of a dingy warehouse.

But there they were, inches from each other, pressed together in a room that only allowed a foot or two of space between them to undress. The shower was even smaller than that.

It wasn't a deterrent for Dimitri, it seemed. He reached around the plastic shower curtain and turned the water on, steam enveloping them almost immediately. If Arlo had thought it would offer some kind of shield to his naked body, he was very wrong. He could see Dimitri just fine, couldn't tear his eyes away as he peeled his shirt over his head and let it drop to the floor.

Arlo swallowed hard, his pulse drumming in his throat. His gaze roamed, taking in Dimitri's muscled chest and the ridged planes of his perfect belly. Arlo trapped his lower lip between his teeth before he said something stupid like, 'marry me,' but he was certain his face said it all.

Dimitri's gaze locked on his with a slow smirk as he made a show of stripping the rest of the way down. Arlo's mouth was a desert, his heart slamming against his ribcage as he took it all in. Holy fuck. Dimitri was very…proportional. His cock jutted up against his belly, hard and flushed, because of Arlo.

Arlo inhaled sharply as reality crashed in on him. In all the times he'd fantasized about the two of them together, he'd never imagined it would be after one of the most brutal beatings of his life. The split lip was nothing compared to what lay below the fabric—just another sign of how truly explosive Holden's fury had been that night. He usually focused on just the parts nobody else saw, but that night, Arlo had dared to question if Holden would ever acknowledge out loud that he was gay. Holden had spent the night showing Arlo just how much he hated being questioned.

Humiliation washed over him. He wanted to be naked with Dimitri, wanted to feel his tongue, his fingers, his everything, really. But as soon as his clothes came off, Dimitri would see exactly how badly he'd allowed Holden to treat him.

Sweat beaded at his hairline, but he couldn't bring

himself to undress. He stood frozen. At least he wasn't cold anymore. Arlo would hate to get away with murder only to die from hypothermia. He startled as Dimitri took a step closer, tugging Arlo's already abused lip free of the prison of his teeth.

"They're waiting for our clothes out there," he reminded, reaching for the hem of Arlo's shirt.

Arlo clenched Dimitri's wrists, keeping him from completing the task. "Wait," he begged breathlessly. Dimitri frowned but paused. "I just need you to know…it's bad."

"What's bad?" Dimitri asked.

Arlo swallowed the sudden lump in his throat. "The bruises. They're bad, but they look worse than they are. Okay? They don't hurt much or anything."

Dimitri's face was a thunderstorm as he gently pulled free of Arlo's hands before tugging his shirt over his head and dropping it to the pile between them. Dimitri's nostrils flared, his jaw tightening until the muscle ticked. Any erection Arlo had disappeared as Dimitri took in the array of bruises at various stages of healing.

Arlo closed his eyes. It was ugly. They were ugly. So fucking ugly.

"Jesus," Dimitri whispered, gentle hands sweeping along his battered torso. "What did he do to you?"

Tears slipped down his cheeks. "I told you it was bad."

Dimitri's fingertips skimmed his waistband, teasing just beneath it as he reached for his button and zipper. When Arlo opened his eyes, Dimitri was on his knees before him. He picked up Arlo's leg, removing one shoe, then the other, before once more reaching for the fastening of Arlo's jeans.

Arlo didn't stop him, just lifted his legs so Dimitri could free him of his clothes. He fought the urge to cover himself. There was really no time. Arlo's mouth was slack as Dimitri's thumbs swept along his hip bones before he leaned forward to kiss the spot just above his belly button.

Arlo's cock twitched. Dimitri's gaze met his, and the sight of him on his knees had all the blood rushing from his head to his dick fast enough to make him dizzy. Dimitri buried his face in the spot where his thigh met his hip, his breath rustling the curls there. Arlo couldn't stop the whine that escaped.

Dimitri's large hands ran from the backs of Arlo's thighs to cup his ass. "I should have stepped in weeks ago," he muttered, dropping kisses to the bruises on his ribs and belly. "I should have killed him," he growled. "I should have told somebody."

Arlo shook his head. "Please, I didn't want anybody to know. It was too embarrassing."

"You did nothing wrong," Dimitri said vehemently.

"Would you have let somebody do this to you?" Arlo countered, tugging Dimitri's head back.

Dimitri appeared to think about it. "Yeah. You. I'd let you hurt me if you wanted to. I'd let you do pretty much anything to me if I'm being honest."

Arlo's breath left him in a whoosh at the wet rasp of Dimitri's tongue licking a line from the spot just above his now rock-hard cock to his belly button. Arlo's fingers clenched in Dimitri's hair, desperate for something to hold on to. "What are you doing?"

"I don't know," Dimitri rasped. "I can't help it. You smell so fucking good right here. It's making me crazy. I've wanted you for so fucking long."

Before Arlo could plan a response, there was a knock on the door and Noah's timid voice said, "Your change of clothes is outside the door. If you're…um, busy…you can just leave your clothes in there. I can grab them later, or whatever."

Arlo started to say, 'thank you,' but the words became a soft cry of surprise as Dimitri swallowed him down, the tight suction of his mouth causing Arlo's knees to buckle. Dimitri's grip on his ass was the only thing keeping him upright.

He shot his hand out to catch on the wall beside the shower. The shower they still weren't in yet.

Arlo wasn't about to point that out, though. His eyelids fluttered as Dimitri's mouth worked over him until it felt as if flames licked along his nerve endings, sending pleasure pulsing through him.

Arlo tried to stifle the sounds pouring from his lips, but when Dimitri took his cock in hand and jerked himself in time with the long, sure pull of his lips, Arlo didn't know how. It was too fucking good. His mouth felt so good.

"Oh, fuck. Oh, fuck, " Arlo chanted breathlessly.

Dimitri's fingers dug into Arlo's ass cheek as he took him impossibly deep, swallowing around him until Arlo wondered if anybody had ever died from ecstasy. "Stop. You have to stop," Arlo warned. "I'm so close. I can't stop myself. You feel too fucking good."

Dimitri didn't stop, didn't even slow his movements. Heat sparked along Arlo's spine, his orgasm barreling towards him like a bullet train until his breath punched from him and he flooded Dimitri's mouth. Dimitri swallowed it down, nursing every drop from Arlo's cock until he hissed, his body too sensitive.

Even after Dimitri pulled off, he didn't stand. He just pressed his forehead to Arlo's hipbone, working himself with purpose, before he bit down on the fleshy part of Arlo's hip, his body going rigid as he spilled his release onto the pile of clothes and the concrete floor below.

After a minute, he stood, walking Arlo backwards into the shower stall and under the scalding water before capturing his mouth in a filthy kiss that left Arlo sucking the taste of himself off Dimitri's tongue. They continued to kiss as they soaped each other, Dimitri's fingers lingering between the cleft of Arlo's ass for much longer than necessary. Not that he was complaining.

When the water cooled, Dimitri turned it off, taking the single oversized white towel from the rack and drying first Arlo, then himself. Arlo wasn't sure exactly what he'd expected as far as spare clothes went, but it wasn't the fitted black pants, graphic tee, and cardigan that sat outside the door. They were a little snug but not so much that Arlo would complain about it.

Adam had been right. His clothes were couture. The jeans Dimitri donned were Armani, the hoodie Chanel. He looked exceptionally good. So good that, for a moment,

Arlo forgot about the dead body in the trunk or that he'd killed somebody. No, not just somebody. A fucking federal judge's son.

"Hey, don't get too in your head about this," Dimitri said. "We're going to be okay."

"We should have been somewhere public an hour ago," Arlo reminded him.

"It's not when we get there," Dimitri assured him. "It's making sure people notice we are there."

"Where are we going to go where people will notice us?"

Dimitri gave him a smug look. "Oh, I know just the place."

Arlo frowned. "And you think this place will be busy enough to establish an alibi?"

Dimitri brushed fingers through Arlo's damp hair. "Stay nice and close, keep looking at me the way you are right now, and I promise, nobody will forget we were there."

Unease trickled along Arlo's spine. "Where?"

Dimitri grinned. "You'll see."

Arlo was not a party person. Most days, he was barely a person. His idea of a good time was walking around a bookstore or playing video games on his futon. Maybe he was riding the post-orgasm bliss, but of all the things he thought he and Dimitri might do to create an alibi, this one had never occurred to him.

Arlo's stomach dropped when Dimitri parked illegally across the street from the giant white two-story home with its immense columns and black shutters. It wasn't the house that threw him, but the letters painted over the entrance signifying the Sigma Chi fraternity. "Please, tell me we're not going in there."

Arlo hated all of fraternity row, but the Sigma Chi's were the worst of the worst. Or maybe they were just the guys Arlo saw most often. They would swarm the coffee shop every day to take up space, buying just enough coffee to keep them from being booted for loitering. He didn't know how Dimitri tolerated them. They spent their time shooting spitballs at each other while calling each other 'bro' and lying about how many girls they banged.

They were just like Holden. Arlo hadn't liked Holden either, but he'd been so desperate for him to want him, to like him, to accept him. Arlo definitely needed to go back to therapy. Maybe Holden was right. Arlo was still this great big sucking hole of neediness, constantly looking for the worst people to fill him up.

He shook the thought away. Holden was dead, and Arlo didn't have time for the breakdown he truly deserved. He had to get away with murder first. He looked at Dimitri, hoping he could convince him to come up with a Plan B, or C, or D. He would be fine with any plan that didn't involve letters written in Greek.

"We need to be remembered, right?" Dimitri asked.

Arlo sighed. He couldn't handle a house full of Holdens, not with the original one still stuffed in his car in the middle of the garage where Dimitri had sucked him off just thirty minutes before.

"I hate Greek life."

Dimitri arched a brow. "I'm Greek and you seem to like me just fine."

Arlo cast a sullen glance towards the house where guys in boat shoes and board shorts were spilling from the house onto the porch, yelling and laughing. It was forty fucking degrees outside. "Those assholes treat me like I'm a servant."

Dimitri leaned across the seat to cup Arlo's cheek, turning him so they were eye to eye. "And that's why they're going to take notice of us. I've been to hundreds of these parties. Do you know how many times I've brought a date?"

Arlo soured. "Is this supposed to be making me feel better?"

Dimitri grinned, leaning forward and biting the tip of Arlo's nose in a weirdly affectionate gesture. "None. I've never brought a single date here. Do you know why?"

"Because Mandy would have skinned them alive and worn them as an accessory?" Arlo muttered.

Dimitri snickered. "No."

"Because it's a house full of homophobic douchebags?" Arlo quipped.

Dimitri barked out a laugh. "No. Well, maybe, but I don't think so. They know I'm gay. They don't give a fuck."

Dimitri ran his knuckles along Arlo's cheekbone. "I've never brought a date because there's been nobody for me but you since the day I met you, almost eighteen years ago."

Arlo arched a brow, mouth flattening. "You're saying you've never been with anybody? Ever?"

Dimitri's forehead wrinkled. He looked like he was

attempting to do complex math. Then his eyes went wide. "Oh! You mean, like, sex? Oh, no. I've had lots of sex. But not with anybody I gave a shit about. I was just killing time until you came to your senses and realized I was the only one for you."

Arlo's brows knitted together. "How was I supposed to do that when you never once showed any interest in me?"

Dimitri shook his head like Arlo was ridiculous. "What are you talking about? How many shifts did I switch with Remi so that I could work with you? How many parties did I blow off so I could hang out at the shop while you worked?" Dimitri asked.

Arlo shook his head, exasperated. "I have no idea, Dimitri. How many?"

Dimitri smiled at Arlo's irritation, kissing his pouting mouth. "A lot. So many that even Remi realized how into you I am. He makes fun of me for it all the time."

Arlo made a mental note to kick Remi's ass for keeping that knowledge to himself. Arlo had spent countless hours whining to Remi about how much he liked Dimitri and he'd never once spilled this very pertinent piece of information. What the fuck? He thought they were friends.

"Well, that only works if I have all the information. You could have just asked me out, you know."

Dimitri cocked his head, giving Arlo a look. "You're never single. Ever. You've been with one guy after another since I started working there four years ago."

His words felt like a blow to the diaphragm, knocking the air from his lungs. "Wow."

Dimitri shook his head. "What?"

"One guy after another?" Arlo repeated, voice dull.

"I'm not insulting you."

"I feel pretty fucking insulted," Arlo managed, looking back out the window, his chest tight.

"Don't do that. Look at me." Arlo forced himself to turn and face him. "When was the last time you were single? Seriously."

Arlo stopped short. He'd started dating Holden as soon as he'd split with Jimmy. Before Jimmy, it was Derek… Jimmy's lab partner. Had Arlo really not been single in four years?

Arlo shook his head. "I'm sorry."

"For what?" Dimitri asked.

Arlo gestured helplessly. "I don't know. I just feel like I'm doing this all wrong."

Dimitri's brows drew together. "Doing what wrong? Us? You can't do us wrong. I'm not like them. I'm sure you've heard that before, but I would never hurt you." He gave a suggestive eyebrow wiggle. "I mean, unless you asked me to."

Arlo rolled his eyes but couldn't stop the smile that stretched across his face. "You owe me big time for this. And I'm never doing this again."

At least, Arlo fucking hoped so. He was not cut out for a life of crime. It was too stressful. He wanted to be done with stressful. He was far too tired for this.

"Well, with any luck, we won't commit any more murders together that require us to come up with alibis."

"You realize that implies there might come a time when one of us might commit a murder separately," Arlo said.

Dimitri leaned forward and kissed him deep, murmuring against his lips, "Well, you have a pretty bad temper. There's no telling what might set you off. You're a very, very dangerous guy."

Arlo let himself get lost in Dimitri's kisses. A heavy fist suddenly pounded on the glass, startling Arlo. He jumped back, looking towards the window just in time to see a group of people continuing their walk down the sidewalk. Yeah, he really fucking hated fraternity row.

"Should we be parked illegally after we just committed murder?" Arlo whispered, as if people might suddenly be listening.

"Yes. If we're lucky, campus police will ticket us and we'll have a police-issued alibi," Dimitri said.

Arlo surged forward and smashed their lips together once more. "You're great at this."

"I'm going to take that as a compliment, even though I'm not entirely sure it is one," Dimitri hedged.

"Text your mom the location so she can fudge the GPS data."

Dimitri chuckled. "You're pretty good at this, too."

"Yeah, yeah," Arlo said, waving off the compliment. "Promise me we can leave in an hour."

"One hour."

"And promise me you won't make me talk to your fratty, douchey friends."

"I promise," Dimitri said dutifully.

"And if Mandy starts rubbing on you like a cat in heat, I will throw hands."

"Noted."

SEVEN

Dimitri held Arlo's hand as they walked around to the back of the frat house. The easiest way to make people think they'd been there a while was to not walk through the front door and announce their arrival.

The backyard wasn't nearly as full as the front porch and the yard which was littered with cups, bottles, and assorted accessories like half deflated beach balls and rusted lawn darts.

The icy air ensured that no smell emanated from the wall of overflowing trash cans lining the house, leaving only the crisp smell of wood burning where various couples shared Adirondack chairs around a firepit. Dimitri picked up a discarded solo cup off the porch railing, peering into it.

"If you drink that, I will most definitely vomit," Arlo promised, horrified.

Dimitri snickered. "Take it."

"Is this a hazing ritual? I would rather get dysentery on the Oregon Trail than drink this."

"Stop being difficult," Dimitri said, forcing the cup

into his hand before draping an arm around Arlo's slight shoulders and gathering him close. He tugged his phone free, pulling up the camera app and putting it in selfie mode. "Kiss my cheek."

Arlo timidly rose on tip-toe to do as he asked. Dimitri turned at the last minute, snapping the picture just as their lips touched, then another as he pulled away. He grinned as he looked at the pictures. They both looked happy, gazing at each other like they were each other's whole worlds.

Arlo was his fucking world. Always had been. Arlo seemed to feel the same way. Part of Dimitri was mad at himself for not shooting his shot four years ago, before men had trampled all over Arlo's heart…and his body. He could have saved Arlo so much pain. Nobody would ever put a hand on Arlo ever again, not without losing a limb for their efforts.

But, for now, it was about establishing a paper trail to keep them from a murder rap. Dimitri loaded the pictures he'd just taken to Instagram, adding a bunch of bullshit hashtags. **#collegelife #fratwars #beerpong #sigmachiordie #boyfriends #couple #partnerincrime**

Arlo snorted as he peered over Dimitri's arm. "Partner in crime? What? #BonnieandClyde was too on the nose?"

Dimitri grinned. "Hey, we want people to take notice. Besides, who would hashtag something like that if they really did just commit a crime?"

"Other than you?" Arlo countered.

"Yeah, other than me," Dimitri teased, taking the used cup from Arlo and setting it aside. "Come on, let's go inside and get this over with."

Arlo grimaced. "I don't want to go in there, but I can't feel my fingers."

Dimitri steered him towards the back door and then wrapped his arms around him from behind, threading their fingers together as he buried his face against his neck. Arlo sagged against him. He trusted Dimitri to take care of him. That shouldn't make his dick hard, but it did. Arlo was his. Just his. And he'd protect him with violence if necessary.

Arlo tilted his head to let Dimitri nuzzle his neck. "This is nice and all, but how are we going to get from here to there if you're holding me hostage?"

The door opened in front of them as a group of half dressed partiers staggered out into the cold, the alcohol clearly numbing them to the air, which was so icy they could see their breath. "Like this."

Arlo shriek laughed as Dimitri picked him up from behind, carrying him through the doorway as one of the drunken girls said, "Aww."

Inside, the living room was a crush of people, some gathered into a large great room, dancing, some crowded into the kitchen around a keg, and others playing beer pong in the dining room.

People knowing they were there wouldn't be a problem. It was like watching people do the wave at a football game, only this time the wave was a hundred drunk college students noticing Dimitri had arrived at the party and that he had a boy in his arms.

"You know that part of the movie where there's, like, a record scratch and then everybody stops and stares?" Arlo asked softly. "We're living that part. I hate that part."

Dimitri held him tighter. "They're just surprised to see me here with somebody. I told you. I've never brought a date before. That's all it is. I promise."

Arlo scoffed, attempting to crane his head over his shoulder to look at Dimitri. "You're a terrible liar."

Dimitri snorted. "I'm an excellent liar. Trust me. This is the best thing that could happen to us." He released his hold on him but took Arlo's hand, weaving through a crowd that parted like the Red Sea but then quickly forgot them.

Dimitri spotted a shaved head and broad shoulders in the kitchen. Jason. He headed that way, thinking Arlo would feel safer among friends. Jason was at the tap, pouring a beer into a solo cup. He did an almost comical double take when he realized Dimitri had his arm around Arlo.

He frowned. "'Sup, man? I thought you couldn't make it?"

Dimitri shrugged. "Arlo said we could come, so here we are."

Jason had the cup halfway to his lips when he paused, looking back and forth between the two of them. "Arlo said you could come? Like, he gave you permission?"

Dimitri shrugged. "I mean, he's my boyfriend. If he doesn't like parties, I don't like parties."

Jason blinked rapidly, as if attempting to process this completely new information. Dimitri didn't blame him. They had traveled in the same circles since freshman year and Dimitri had never introduced him to a boyfriend before. Dimitri had never had a boyfriend before.

Silence stretched between them until Arlo stiffened.

"Let's just go. I knew people would be weird about me being here."

Jason appeared to snap out of whatever stupor Dimitri had caused. "Nah, man. You're good. You're both good. Of course, you are. We're not homophobes. Like, do you. Have a beer." He looked at Arlo with wide eyes. "Do you drink beer? We have wine and jello shots!" he said excitedly before frowning, his head on a swivel as he looked around. "Somewhere."

"I'm good," Arlo said, sounding faintly amused.

They went to leave when Jason snagged Dimitri's arm, tugging him around. "Wait, does Mandy know you two are a thing?"

Dimitri shook his head. "Arlo wasn't comfortable telling anyone before tonight."

There wasn't anything to tell before tonight, but that was for Dimitri to know and Jason to never find out. His face lit up like a kid on Christmas morning. He turned to a guy who was currently standing between the legs of a blonde perched on the kitchen counter. "Josh, watch the keg. I got something to do." To Dimitri, he said, "Come with me."

Dimitri looked at Arlo, who looked as suspicious as Dimitri felt, but he just shrugged. Dimitri followed behind Jason, once more weaving through groups of drunken revelers into what had once been a library when this was a normal house and not a frat house. An enormous wraparound leather couch hugged two walls, and Mandy sat on the arm, leaning over a burly football player who appeared to talk directly into her cleavage.

"Hey, Mandy," Jason called. "Look who showed up."

Mandy's head snapped up, her face contorted like it irritated her that Jason had interrupted her, but then she saw Dimitri and a shark-like grin spread across her face, the guy on the couch forgotten. She rose, regal as a queen, smoothing the skirt of her green dress, hips swaying as she crossed to where they stood. Dimitri wondered if she thought that was seductive. Maybe it was to straight dudes. What did he know?

"He brought his *boyfriend*," Jason tacked on gleefully, emphasizing the word, as he pushed Arlo forward. "You remember Arlo, right? From the coffee shop."

Mandy stopped short like Jason had dropped a dead rat at her feet, her nose wrinkling. "I'm sorry, what?"

Jason feigned confusion. "Yeah, didn't you know he and Arlo were a thing?" he said, as if that wasn't information he himself had learned just sixty seconds prior to this meeting. "For a while now. They're really cute together, no?"

Dimitri wasn't sure what he was witnessing. He'd always assumed Jason and Mandy were friends. They were always together. They had the same circle of friends. But, Dimitri did as well, so maybe none of them were really friends, just victims of circumstance and geography. Or, in Dimitri's case, a meddling mother determined the world didn't know of his secret psychopathy.

Mandy raked her gaze over Arlo from head to toe before dismissing him entirely to focus on Dimitri, arching one overly manicured brow. "You're dating…him?"

Dimitri tilted his head, well aware there were people

attempting to covertly film their encounter. Mandy's crush on Dimitri was hardly a secret, but then, neither was Dimitri's sexual orientation. "Yeah. Arlo and I have been together for a while now. Why?"

She raised her chin, her arms crossing beneath her breasts. "Because it makes no sense. Look at you"—she waved a hand—"and then look at him."

Arlo stiffened. Dimitri's whole body grew hot, an uncharacteristic rage rolling over him. He pulled Arlo back against him once more, cradling his body, as if he could deflect all of Mandy's nastiness.

Dimitri dropped all pretenses, letting the mask of normalcy fall away, his voice a low growl as he said, "What did you just say?"

He could hear people murmuring throughout the crowd. He'd known she was going to throw a tantrum, but it never occurred to him she would attack Arlo because she thought he didn't meet some arbitrary set of standards she'd decided were a thing. He wouldn't stand there and let her humiliate him publicly, not even to secure an alibi.

Mandy's smug demeanor cracked, some part of her clearly sensing Dimitri wasn't who she thought he was, her voice wavering. "I'm just saying, you two hardly run in the same circles. That's all. I didn't know *that* would be your type, I guess."

Dimitri dropped his lips to the top of Arlo's head. "*That*? You mean sweet, smart, sexy as fuck?"

"You forgot good in bed," Arlo said helpfully.

Dimitri grinned. "My bad, babe. He's fucking incredible

in bed."

Once more, her face contorted in disgust. Before Dimitri could say anything, Arlo said, "You good, sweetie? You look a little…emotionally constipated."

Dimitri sucked his lips in to keep from laughing. The rest of the crowd wasn't so kind. He could hear snickers from all sides of the small sitting room.

Whatever timidity Dimitri had scared into Mandy a moment ago disappeared. She cocked her hip, sneering. "I just didn't see Dimitri settling for some skinny, meek little twink. That is the term for scrawny little gays, right? Twink?" she asked, enunciating the last word.

Dimitri pictured wrapping his hands around Mandy's throat and squeezing until her eyes popped from their sockets. This had been a huge mistake. A bar fight in the worst part of town would have been less painful than this. He should have listened to Arlo.

Arlo stepped free from Dimitri's arms. "Oh, are we giving vocabulary lessons? Because I have one for you as well. Mandy: sad little hag who chases after clearly gay men because she thinks her vagina is so fucking magical that she can fuck them straight. News flash: it's not."

Mandy's mouth fell open, her face flushing. She started to retort, but Arlo held up a hand.

"Oh, or wait, maybe it's the other meaning of Mandy. Girl who brags about acting in the B movie, *Mean Girls 3*, but fails to mention that she was so insignificant and stereotypical that she's simply credited as basic bitch number 2."

"Oh, shit," somebody muttered from somewhere behind them.

Dimitri hadn't known Arlo knew about that. He shouldn't be surprised. Mandy's minuscule part in a major motion picture was one of the biggest arrows in her quiver of superiority. He watched as her mouth opened and closed like a fish gasping for air.

Arlo tilted his head, his eyes narrowing, as he now looked *her* up and down. "Anything else you want to say, Botox Barbie? Because I can do this all night."

Tears formed in Mandy's eyes, but before a single one could fall, she stuck her nose in the air. "Whatever. You're not worth it."

As she stormed off, Arlo wiggled his fingers in a mockery of a wave. "Bye now."

Dimitri stepped forward to comfort Arlo but never got the chance. Jason enveloped Arlo in a bear hug, lifting him off his feet and shaking him as he shouted, "That. Was. Awesome."

When he set him down, he pointed directly into Arlo's startled face with one fat finger. "You're cool. You're invited to party with us any fucking time." To Dimitri, he said, "I'm not gay, bro. But you're right, that *was* sexy as fuck."

Then he left, leaving Arlo and Dimitri in a sea of strange faces, who quickly lost interest now that the battle of wits had ended. "Well, you made a good impress…" Dimitri's words died as he saw Arlo's wide, terrified eyes. "Hey, you good?"

He watched Arlo's Adam's apple bob as he swallowed hard. "I need air. I need to get out of here."

Dimitri nodded. "Okay. Let's go."

Dimitri steered him out the front door to the now deserted porch. He didn't stop until they were at the sidewalk. "What's wrong? What happened? Was it what Mandy said?"

Arlo shook his head jerkily, shivering. Maybe from the cold, maybe from fear. "Jason."

Dimitri's eyes went wide. Jason shouting in Arlo's face, grabbing him without permission. "Did he scare you?"

Arlo flinched at Dimitri's words. "I'm not—s-scared. I know he wasn't trying to hurt me, but my body isn't getting the message. I think I'm having a panic attack. I feel like my insides are shaking. Can we please go home? I don't even care if I go to prison. Just take me home."

"My home or yours?" Dimitri asked, guiding him back to the car, mentally fist pumping when he saw the white rectangular ticket tucked under the windshield wiper. Alibi secured.

"Yours. I don't want to go back to my depressing apartment."

"Okay, we'll go back to *my* depressing apartment," Dimitri joked, relieved when Arlo gave a watery smile.

Once he had Arlo tucked into the passenger seat and his seatbelt on, he ran around to the driver's side, sliding in and turning over the engine so the heat kicked on. But he didn't take off right away. "I'm sorry."

Arlo's gaze jerked towards him. "What?"

"I'm sorry."

Arlo frowned. "Why?"

Dimitri stopped short. "I'm not sure. I know I should be sorry, right? I did something that got you hurt. I should feel bad about that."

"But you don't?" Arlo asked.

Dimitri shook his head, bewildered. "I don't feel bad, exactly. I feel…angry. Like I wanted to hurt her. I wanted to squeeze the breath from her body and watch the life drain from her eyes."

Arlo lifted his head, expression bemused. "Easy, killer. One dead body is enough for today, I think."

"Does it scare you?" Dimitri asked softly. "Do I scare you?"

Arlo gave a soft laugh. "No. Maybe it makes me a shitty person, but I like that you want to kill people for me. Does that scare you?" he countered.

"No. I feel relieved. If I could be sorry, I would be sorry that Mandy was such a bitch to you. I should have seen it coming. I just wanted to show you off."

"You wanted to show me off," Arlo echoed.

Dimitri frowned. "Is that, like—not misogynistic but—is that, like, not respecting your autonomy or something? My brain doesn't really think in terms of, like, societal norms. I don't want to offend you or make you feel bad."

Arlo's face flushed in the dim glow of the overhead light. "Nobody has ever wanted to 'show me off.' I've been a dirty little secret for so long that I don't even know how to be out in public, and I'm not even the one in the closet."

"You'll never be that to me," Dimitri promised.

Arlo smiled, lifting his hand to run his fingers over Dimitri's cheek. "Mandy has been making me miserable for four years. It's like she secretly knew I was into you or something and wanted me to know I never stood a chance. I knew what we were getting into. I just wasn't ready for Jason's…enthusiasm."

Dimitri licked his lower lip. "I can't promise I won't be just as enthusiastic once I get you back to my apartment." He leaned forward, capturing Arlo's mouth in a kiss, darting his tongue quickly inside. "You know, where my bedroom is."

"And your bed?" Arlo murmured.

"Yeah," Dimitri said against his lips.

Arlo's hand ran along the inside of Dimitri's thigh, gasping when he felt how hard he was. "Then we should probably hurry."

EIGHT
ARLO

It seemed strange that, in all the times he and Dimitri had been dancing around each other, Arlo had never been to Dimitri's apartment. Not even as friends. Dimitri had called it depressing, but it looked wonderfully normal to Arlo. There was a small kitchen, a tiny table sat nearby with two chairs, and there was a decent-sized living room with a comfortable-looking sofa and a big tv.

Arlo's apartment was half the size, and he had to cook everything in a microwave or by using a hot plate. And his manager had control of the thermostat, so Arlo spent most fall and winter nights buried under a dozen blankets.

Dimitri's apartment was tidy with everything in its place, except for the shoes Dimitri slipped off beside the door. Arlo did the same, butterflies taking flight in his belly as Dimitri smiled at him, pulling him towards the closed door to the left.

He was really going to have sex with Dimitri. *More sex,* he corrected, goosebumps erupting along his skin as he remembered the heat of Dimitri's mouth on him. When the door closed behind them, Arlo reached for the hem of his shirt.

Dimitri's hands gripped his wrists gently, just as Arlo had done to him earlier. "Whatcha doin'?"

Arlo frowned. "Getting naked. Isn't that how this usually works?"

Arlo supposed they could leave their clothes on. It wouldn't be the first time some guy just wanted access to the only part they found worthy of their attention. He'd thought Dimitri was different. He'd called Arlo his boyfriend. In public. Maybe that was all for show?

Dimitri sat on the edge of the bed and pulled Arlo close, resting his chin on Arlo's diaphragm, gazing up at him to ask, "You got another date after me?"

Arlo flustered. "What? No."

Dimitri grinned up at him. "I'm teasing."

"Oh," Arlo said, voice dull.

Arlo was suddenly hyper-aware of every atom in his own body, but it felt like he'd lost control of it. He was nervous, and there was a panic setting in that hadn't been there moments before. He was ruining this. He was ruining everything.

"Are you okay?" Dimitri asked, voice gentle.

Arlo shook his head. "No. I'm not. I have no idea what we're doing here, what *I'm* doing here."

Dimitri frowned. "I thought we were both pretty clear about what we wanted in the car? But if you don't want to do this, we don't have to."

Arlo's heart was slamming into his ribs. Everything was overwhelming him. "I know *what* we're doing, I just don't know *how* we're doing it."

"How?" Dimitri asked.

Arlo flushed to the roots of his hair, and he closed his eyes before saying, miserably, "I don't know how you want me. Like, you don't want me to take off my clothes, so, like, do you just want a quick and dirty hookup? Am I supposed to do…something? I don't know what to do."

Dimitri pulled Arlo down until he perched on his lap. Once they were eye to eye, Dimitri said, "Hi."

"Hi," Arlo managed, voice trembling.

"I need to be clear about something," Dimitri said.

Arlo's heart sank, tears springing to his eyes. This was always how it started, the dreaded, 'Can we talk?' speech. Old conversations dialed up in his thoughts, replaying in his head.

"I'm not looking for anything serious. I thought you knew that."

"People don't know I'm out yet. That's all. Don't be so needy."

"My friends just wouldn't get your vibe. You're kind of a downer."

"It's for my career. You understand, don't you, beautiful?"

"I want you in all the ways."

"What?" Arlo asked, certain that he'd imagined Dimitri's answer.

Dimitri gently captured Arlo's wrists behind his back, leaning in to lick his way into his mouth in a way that was both sweet and dirty, grinding their hips together so Arlo could feel how hard he was.

"You heard me," Dimitri said between kisses. "I have every intention of having you any way you'll let me, and, believe me, I've had a lot of time to think about that. But I thought maybe I could just strip you naked first. I really want to see you naked in my bed." He buried his face against Arlo's neck. "Would that be okay?"

"Yeah," Arlo said, breathless.

Dimitri pulled back to study his face. "You still look unsure."

Arlo swallowed the lump in his throat. "I'm not unsure about you. I just want you to enjoy this and I feel like I'm ruining it for you."

"You get that we're both supposed to enjoy this, right?" Dimitri asked. Not in Arlo's experience. There was a very specific hierarchy of needs and Arlo's always came last or not at all. Usually, the latter. "Jesus," Dimitri whispered. "You really don't know that. Do you?"

Arlo's face grew hot, shame burning through him like acid. It took every ounce of self-control not to bolt for the door. "Should I leave? I feel like I already screwed this up."

"Arlo?"

Was it possible to die of embarrassment? "Yeah?"

Dimitri kissed his lips, his jaw, then nuzzled the spot behind his ear. "Can I take your clothes off? Please?"

Dimitri still wanted to do this? That seemed all but impossible. But this night was full of a million impossible things. Arlo had broken up with Holden. Arlo had *murdered* Holden. He'd gone to a frat party, had stood in a warehouse full of killers. Dimitri had gone to his knees for Arlo in that same warehouse. What was one more impossible thing?

Arlo gave a stilted nod. "Yeah."

Dimitri's grin was almost feral. He released Arlo's wrists to peel his shirt over his head, tossing it blindly behind him. His arms slipped around Arlo's back to grip his shoulders, holding him still while he ran his tongue up the center of his chest before dipping into the hollow of his throat.

Arlo's cock strained against the zipper of his too tight borrowed pants. He couldn't stop himself from rolling his hips against Dimitri, who gave a pleased rumble, pulling him closer. Each time Dimitri ground his hips against him, flames licked along his nerve endings. It felt too fucking good.

Arlo gave a broken moan as Dimitri dipped his head, taking one hard nipple into his mouth, sucking it gently before tugging on it with his teeth. Arlo buried his hand in Dimitri's hair, guiding him to his other nipple, desperate to feel him everywhere.

Arlo ran his hands up under Dimitri's hoodie, his fingers feeling their way along the defined ridges of his abs, earning another noise of approval. But when he reached for Dimitri's hoodie, Dimitri batted his hands away. "Uh-uh. This is about you."

Arlo frowned. "Isn't it about us?"

Dimitri looked him in the eye. "We have our whole lives to make it about us. This one time can't it just be about you? I want to be the one who makes you feel good."

Arlo once more sucked his bottom lip between his teeth, and Dimitri tugged it free, leaning in to run his tongue along the swollen flesh.

Why was it so hard for Arlo to just say yes? They didn't have time for that rabbit hole of unresolved trauma tonight. "Yeah. Okay. But I want you inside me?"

Again, that near feral snarl escaped Dimitri's lips as his hands dropped to Arlo's ass, dragging him close to grind their cocks together in a way that had them both groaning. "That's the plan. Now, stand up."

Arlo lurched to his feet, clinging to Dimitri's shoulders as he rid him of the rest of his clothes. Once he was naked, Arlo's nerves took over again. There was nothing more vulnerable than being the only naked person in the room. As impossible as it was, some small niggling part of Arlo whispered that Dimitri was just luring him into a false sense of security. That he wanted him comfortable so he could tear him down.

He pushed the intrusive thought away as Dimitri stood, his hands roaming over Arlo's now bare ass, his fingers dipping into his crease like he just couldn't resist. "On the bed. On your stomach."

Arlo's mouth was a desert as he crawled onto the bed. Dimitri's well-worn comforter was cool against his overheated skin. He waited, legs slightly parted, expecting the heavy weight of Dimitri's body to press him into the mattress, the rough sting of dry fingers pushing into him.

Instead, warm oil drizzled over one foot. Arlo smirked as he saw Dimitri holding a bottle of baby oil. What college student had baby oil? Dimitri. After that, all thought dissolved, leaving only sensation as Dimitri's powerful hands rubbed and kneaded his way up one of Arlo's legs and down the other.

If Dimitri was hoping to relax him, it definitely wasn't working. Arlo didn't think his dick—trapped between his body and the comforter—had ever been so hard. He was sure he was making a mess of Dimitri's bed. Arlo's frustration ratcheted higher with each pass of Dimitri's hands until it felt like he was toying with Arlo, thumbs skimming so close to his balls that he would hold his breath, only to be disappointed when they instead followed under the curve of his ass.

He didn't know how much time passed, his body dancing on a knife's edge of ecstasy and exasperation, but when the bed finally shifted, Dimitri had worked every part of Arlo from his head to his toes until he was just one raw nerve ending, desperate for relief.

Arlo sucked in a breath when Dimitri's large hands gripped his hips, tugging them up just enough to slide his arms beneath. Before Arlo could ask what he was doing, he spread him open, Dimitri's soft tongue licking over him from his balls to his hole.

The sound Arlo made was something between a cry and a moan, but Dimitri must have liked it because he buried his face in the heart of him, his tongue doing things that made Arlo's toes curl and his dick throb.

But it wasn't enough to fill the emptiness inside him. And now, he couldn't even rub himself against the mattress. "I'm good. I'm ready," Arlo promised.

Arlo mourned the loss of Dimitri's talented tongue,

but then teeth nipped playfully at his ass cheek before disappearing. Arlo looked over his shoulder just in time to watch Dimitri strip. He was so fucking beautiful. The living definition of a Greek god.

And he wanted Arlo. Once more, that overwhelming feeling consumed him, but it wasn't a scary feeling. More like anticipation, the culmination of a crush that started when Arlo was too little to understand just how deeply their connection ran.

When Dimitri kneeled between Arlo's open thighs, he dropped his head back to the pillow, certain that if he kept watching, he might shoot his load before Dimitri was even inside.

Slick fingers teased between his cheeks, rubbing over his entrance. Arlo canted his hips, hoping Dimitri would get the message. He sucked in a breath as Dimitri pushed all the way inside. His other hand pulled him apart, and when Arlo risked another glance, he realized Dimitri was watching his finger disappear inside him.

Holy fuck. He couldn't stop himself from rocking back against him, wanting more. Dimitri complied, adding another finger, corkscrewing them inside him in a way that stole Arlo's breath each time he glanced over his prostate.

Arlo no longer cared about embarrassment. He wanted more, wanted all of it. Needed to feel Dimitri's cock slamming home. He couldn't handle the waiting. "Please," he begged.

The butterflies in his belly turned to bees as Dimitri's fingers disappeared and he heard foil tearing. Then Dimitri's body was blanketing over his, his cock settling between his cheeks. Still, he didn't push in, just lazily rocked his hips, his lips pressing against Arlo's ear to whisper, "You sure?"

"Yes," Arlo whispered, frustrated.

Dimitri chuckled, then shifted his weight to one hand, the blunt head of his cock now pressing against Arlo's entrance. He had only a second to familiarize himself with the sensation, and then Dimitri was pushing past that first tight ring of muscle. Arlo hissed at the familiar burning sting as his body adjusted to the invasion.

Once fully seated, Dimitri peppered kisses along his throat, his jawline, bit along the shell of his ear. But he didn't move.

"I'm good," Arlo assured him, wiggling beneath him.

"You sure?" Dimitri asked again.

Arlo scoffed. "I appreciate that you're attempting to be attentive to my needs, but I really need you to fuck me, Dimitri. Damn."

Dimitri laughed at Arlo's tone. His hands then ran along Arlo's arms, threading their fingers together as he came up on his knees, nudging Arlo's thighs farther apart, pulling almost all the way out before slamming back in, making them both groan. "Is that what you need?"

"Fuck. Yes. Please."

Dimitri's fingers tightened around his and then he was moving, fucking into Arlo with hard, slow thrusts that had Arlo's eyes rolling and helpless whimpers falling from his lips each time he drove into him. Dimitri's mouth was everywhere, kissing and sucking at whatever skin he could reach.

Arlo had never really understood when people said sex was intimate. It had never been that for him but more like a chore, an expectation that came with relationships. Something to endure. But he got it now. Dimitri was inside him, on top of him, his breath panting against Arlo's ear, his sweat dripping onto his skin, their bodies moving as one cohesive being, and it was the single most erotic experience of Arlo's life.

He couldn't get enough. Pleasure shot through him each time the head of Dimitri's cock glanced that tiny bundle of nerves. Warmth pooled in his belly. He might actually come untouched. The combined sensation of Dimitri moving inside him and the friction of the cover beneath him on his oversensitive cock was driving him mad.

Dimitri's weight disappeared, though he didn't pull free. He just sank back on his knees, dragging Arlo's hips higher, wrapping his hands around Arlo's narrow waist to drive into him with powerful thrusts that had fireworks exploding behind his eyes. "Oh, fuck. Yes, keep doing that. Please."

Dimitri grunted, somehow pounding into him harder until Arlo's toes were curling and he couldn't stop the breathless cries escaping his lips. He reached beneath him, moaning with relief when he took himself in hand, jerking his aching cock in time with Dimitri's punishing thrusts. It only took three or four pulls, and then Arlo was crying out, spilling his release onto the comforter below.

Dimitri groaned. "Holy fuck, I can feel you coming. You're so fucking tight. Jesus," Dimitri muttered almost to himself. Arlo dropped his head, his fingers curling into the pillows as Dimitri continued to use him, for once finding the experience empowering. He was making Dimitri feel good. Him. Arlo. His body was bringing him pleasure. If he could have grown hard again, he would have.

Dimitri's hips fell off-rhythm, his fingers digging into Arlo's hipbones as he pulled him close, fucking into him with tiny aborted thrusts before grinding his hips against his ass with a hoarse shout. Arlo could feel him coming, could feel his cock throbbing inside him. What would that feel like without the condom between them?

Dimitri became a dead weight, forcing him flat against the mattress as he panted on top of him. Arlo grimaced as he felt Dimitri pull free, shifting to get rid of the condom somewhere over the side of the bed. Arlo couldn't bring himself to care enough about where or how.

When Dimitri fell back onto the mattress, he gathered Arlo against him. "You're all slippery," he said with a laugh.

"Whose fault is that?" Arlo asked, too cum-drunk to worry about monitoring his responses.

"Mine." They lay there for a few minutes before Dimitri asked, "Was it good?"

Arlo glanced up at him, incredulous. "Are you kidding? It was amazing." Dimitri preened. "Was it good for you?" Arlo asked, chest tight.

"It was better than I'd imagined and I have a great imagination."

Arlo wondered if it would ever stop feeling weird that Dimitri wanted him—had seemingly always wanted him— just as much as Arlo wanted him.

"What do we do now?"

"We wait for my mother to contact us. Why don't you take a nap? It's been a long day."

"I thought psychopaths were selfish?" Arlo blurted.

"I'm a well-trained psychopath. My mother has been coaching me on being a good person, a good boyfriend, a good husband, father, and humanitarian since I was five. It takes every ounce of my strength not to be selfish with you."

"I wouldn't mind you being a little selfish with me," Arlo admitted.

Dimitri grinned. "Noted. Get some sleep."

NINE

DIMITRI

The call from his mother came in a few hours before dawn. "Get to the warehouse and wait for further instructions," she said, then disconnected.

Await further instructions. She didn't even sound like his mom anymore. She sounded like his handler. Her disappointment was obvious, and he understood why. She'd sacrificed everything for him, and no matter how much she loved her work, this had to feel like a slap in the face to her.

Would she ever go back to being proud of him, or had this ruined him in her eyes forever? If he could feel regret, would that make her more inclined to forgive him? He needed to fix it, but it would have to be later. After they finished this.

Dimitri glanced down at Arlo curled into a ball beside him. He slept so peacefully, red lips parted as he snored softly. Dimitri couldn't stop himself from dipping his head to brush his lips over Arlo's slack mouth. Arlo made a happy sound at the back of his throat, lips parting for Dimitri, even in sleep. Something flared to life inside Dimitri as he gently rolled Arlo onto his back, deepening the kiss, dick hardening as Arlo's tongue slid over his.

Fuck.

Arlo was so responsive, so open, letting Dimitri take what he wanted, letting him swallow every breathy whimper. Dimitri had been waiting his entire life for this, for Arlo to be just his. He thought Dimitri wasn't selfish, but he was wrong. Dimitri wanted every single part of Arlo—his body, his heart, his soul. He wanted thoughts of him to consume Arlo the way thoughts of Arlo consumed him.

But for that to happen, Arlo had to heal, had to talk to somebody more qualified than Dimitri to process all the shit the universe had dumped on him. But no therapist would ever take Arlo away from him. Not now, not after everything. Even if never seeing Dimitri again was the best thing for Arlo.

Dimitri didn't harbor any murderous impulses, had never longed to unleash the darkest parts of himself on the world at large, but there was darkness in him, a deep, throbbing need to be the center of Arlo's universe. His sole focus.

Did that make him a bad person? Arlo was his entire world. And Dimitri would keep Arlo safe. But he couldn't do that if he wasn't there. He'd already lost eighteen years with him. That was enough. Never again.

When Arlo's hands reached out blindly, Dimitri rolled on top of him, settling between his parted thighs, growling when he realized Arlo was already hard. He rocked his hips against Arlo's, smiling when his lids fluttered open, his arms raising to encircle Dimitri's neck.

"Hi," Arlo said, voice rough with sleep, tugging Dimitri back down, slanting their mouths together, as he wrapped his legs around his waist, locking his ankles just above Dimitri's ass.

They needed to go. His mother was waiting for them to get to the warehouse, but Arlo was rutting against him, making needy little desperate sounds that went straight to Dimitri's already straining dick. There was never any question which route he would choose.

He deepened the kiss, gathering Arlo close, rocking against him with intention. Arlo moaned into his mouth, rising to meet each rolling movement of his hips until the rough catch of skin on skin became a smooth slide, eased by sweat and precum. Dimitri's movements grew frantic until they were no longer kissing, just breathing against each other's lips.

"Oh, fuck," he whispered, when the heat gathered at the base of his spine and he hit that point of no return. "I'm gonna come."

Arlo's heels dug into Dimitri's ass, spurring him on, until his orgasm punched from him and he was spilling between them. He rose just enough to wrap his fist around Arlo's flushed cock, using his cum to jerk him with little finesse, unable to tear his gaze away from Arlo's face. He had his head thrown back, his lids at half-mast as he gazed at Dimitri, fucking up into his tightened fist until he cried out. Dimitri dropped his gaze to watch Arlo come over his fist, working him until he winced.

Dimitri raised cum-covered fingers to his lips, offering them to Arlo. His lips parted to accept Dimitri's offering, not just tasting them but sucking them clean. Christ, that was hot.

Dimitri was half-tempted to leave Holden rotting in the trunk of his car so he could just stay there, learning all the ways he could take Arlo apart. "You're so fucking sexy,"

Arlo flushed, smiling bashfully, before he hid his face behind his hand. "Shut up."

Dimitri pulled his hand away. "I mean it. Sometimes, I just sit and watch you at work, wondering what you'd do if I just pulled you into the back office and fucked you on Maggie's desk."

Arlo flushed. "You'd have to push all her Funko Pop dolls on the floor first."

Dimitri grinned. "I'd risk Maggie's wrath to be inside you."

Their boss had a weird obsession with the little plastic figurines. Dimitri took Arlo's hands in his.

Arlo flushed. "You can't just say stuff like that."

"I can if it's true," Dimitri countered.

Arlo rose up on his forearms. "What time is it?"

"Late…or early, I guess, depending on how you look at it." Dimitri took a deep breath and let it out. "Don't freak out, but my mom called. We need to go back to the warehouse. It's time to finish this."

Dimitri watched Arlo's Adam's apple bob convulsively. But he just nodded, looking resigned.

They didn't shower, just cleaned up in the sink. Arlo pulled his borrowed pants back on, but Dimitri insisted he put on something thicker than the cardigan he'd worn earlier, throwing one of his hoodie's towards him, then tugging a beanie over his head, before changing into black jeans and a hoodie himself. He didn't want to get blood on Adam's couture.

Arlo didn't speak the entire ride back to the garage, just held Dimitri's hand in a death grip while he stared out a window far too obscured by ice to provide much of a view.

When they turned into the industrial park once more, Dimitri said, "If you want me to handle this, I can. You can just meet me in my car when I'm finished getting rid of him."

Arlo shook his head, finally turning to look at Dimitri. "No. No way. The last time you tried to save me, I lost you for years. You can't just keep cleaning up my messes."

Dimitri frowned. "It's our mess. You were defending me. He was trying to kill me."

Arlo gave him a suspicious look. "You probably could have defended yourself," Arlo said. "I just panicked."

Dimitri thought back to that moment. "Honestly, I couldn't get any leverage. If he'd slit my throat, I wouldn't have been able to stop him. You saved me. So, nobody is cleaning up anybody else's messes. We're in this together. Okay?"

Arlo gave a stilted nod. "Yeah. Yeah, okay."

Dimitri scanned the streets, noting not even the homeless roamed at this time of the morning. As they pulled into the parking lot of the warehouse, the anemic glow of the streetlamp was the only light. The windows at the top of the bay door revealed nothing inside but inky blackness.

Dimitri squeezed Arlo's hand one last time before he hopped out of the car and punched in the number to open the place up, jogging back to the car and hopping in while they waited for the door to crawl slowly upward.

Dimitri's headlights revealed the interior a strip at a time. When the door was a quarter of the way open, Dimitri frowned, his heart pounding a little faster. They should have been able to see the tires of the Mercedes. Maybe he'd pulled it farther into the space than he'd thought?

He heard Arlo swallow hard beside him, then felt him grip his wrist. The entire concrete floor was visible now. There was no Mercedes.

Arlo's gaze jerked to Dimitri in confusion. "Where is it?"

Dimitri studied the recesses of the space like it was an optical illusion, like the car had to linger behind some false wall. "I don't know."

Arlo's voice shook as he asked, "Did your mom have it moved?"

Dimitri shook his head. "She would have told me if she'd done that."

Wouldn't she? Maybe she was trying to teach Dimitri some kind of life lesson to make sure he never chose violence again. She had no way of knowing he hadn't chosen violence the first time.

"Well, Holden didn't crawl out of the trunk with a gaping wound in his skull and drive off," Arlo said, his voice climbing. "Did he?" The last part of his sentence sounded desperate, like he was hoping Holden had actually risen from the dead and driven himself home.

"No."

"Do you think the cops found the car and took it? Do you think this is a trap?" Arlo jerked around to look behind them. "Are they watching us?"

Dimitri considered the possibility before dismissing it. "If the cops found the car, this would be a crime scene. We would have seen the lights and heard the sirens a mile away."

"Are you sure?" Arlo asked.

"Yes. I'm positive," he lied.

He picked up his phone from the console between them, pulling up his mother's number and hitting send.

She answered on the second ring. "It took you long enough. Did you stop for breakfast?"

"Did you move the body?" he asked, in lieu of a polite greeting.

There was a long pause on the other side of the line. "What?"

The tone of his mother's voice unnerved him. "Did you move the body? The car? Is this some kind of life lesson? Because, if it is, I think you could have saved it. My life of crime is over."

"Dimitri, what are you talking about?"

Dimitri's stomach churned. "The car… It's gone."

"Gone?" she echoed.

Was this some kind of game? "Disappeared. Evaporated. Dematerialized. Whatever you want to call it, Mom. The car's gone."

"Christ," she muttered almost to herself. "Don't move a

muscle. I'll call you back."

Then his mother hung up on him for the second time that night. When Dimitri glanced at Arlo, he said, "She didn't move the car, did she?"

Dimitri shook his head. "No."

Lights appeared in the rearview mirror, temporarily blinding Dimitri. For a split second, Dimitri thought Arlo was right, that they'd driven right into a sting operation, but he reminded himself that it wouldn't be one cop in an unmarked police car that came for them. Holden was a judge's son. They would have had SWAT there if they knew what they'd done.

Time stretched as the car pulled to a stop dangerously close to their bumper, ensuring they couldn't retreat. Dimitri watched in the side-view mirror as the driver's side door pushed open and a large silhouette in a heavy coat exited, ambling towards them with little urgency.

"What is happening? Who is that?" Arlo snapped.

Dimitri shook his head. "I don't know, but let me do the talking."

Before Arlo could reply, knuckles rapped against the glass. Dimitri cursed himself for not carrying a weapon in his car before he slowly lowered the driver's side window. Of all the things Dimitri expected, it wasn't the young woman's face that appeared behind the frosty windowpane.

She was young, probably not even thirty. She had bright pink hair, and when she stood at her full height, Dimitri realized the woman was not large but heavily pregnant.

What the fuck? "Can we help you?"

"Nope. I'm here to help you." She handed him an envelope. "Go to this address. Don't tell anybody. Especially not your mother."

"What is happening here?" Dimitri asked.

The girl gave him a bright smile, like this was the most normal thing in the world. "Don't waste time with questions I'm not going to answer. I would hurry. It's almost dawn."

With that, she gave a jovial wave and waddled back to her car, slowly pulling away and driving into the night, as much of a mystery as she was when she'd arrived.

"I feel like we've entered the fucking Twilight Zone," Dimitri muttered.

Arlo chewed on his lower lip before asking, "What do we do?"

What could they do? Whoever was on the other side of the note had Holden's car and his body. They held all the cards. They couldn't just forget about it and go home.

"We go to that address. What choice do we have?"

Arlo released a shuddery breath. "None, I guess."

TEN

ARLO

Arlo had plenty of time to cycle through the five stages of grief on their forty-five minute drive from one side of the city to the other. There was something weirdly fitting about driving down a dark, empty interstate together. It felt…final. Fatalistic. Like maybe they were doomed from the start.

He'd tried to convince himself this wasn't happening. That he was dead, and this was hell, and he would now get everything he had coming to him for beating a man's head in with a brick. No matter how much that man deserved it.

Then he'd decided he wasn't dead but in a coma. That none of the night's events had happened. That Holden had beat him into unconsciousness and this was his body shutting down, pumping toxic chemicals into his brain that caused him to have these surreal experiences. It was the only thing that made sense when he thought about the events of the night, both bad and good.

Now, he'd settled into the reality that something had gone terribly, inexplicably sideways during the night—while

Dimitri had buried himself inside him—and whoever was on the other end of that note was planning on blackmailing them or turning them in to the cops. It made the most—and least—amount of sense. What they'd done was surely worthy of blackmail, but neither Arlo nor Dimitri owned anything worthy of payment.

"It's going to be okay," Dimitri said for the hundredth time since they'd gotten back on the road.

"I know," Arlo lied again, giving him what he hoped was a reassuring smile.

Arlo had already decided. He wouldn't let Dimitri go down for this. He wasn't falling on his sword again. Not for him. In the grand scheme of things, his life just wasn't worth the same as Dimitri's.

Dimitri had a mother who loved him, and friends who would miss him, and a shot at an actual future. Arlo only had Dimitri. Nobody would miss him, nobody would mourn him. It made sense for him to own up to what he did and just accept the consequences.

Arlo had already had the best night of his life. He'd had hours with Dimitri, hours in his arms and in his bed. He got to hold the knowledge in his heart that Dimitri had thought about nobody but him for years. That was amazing. Miraculous even. It gave Arlo something to cling to when the thoughts of jail or death gripped his insides again.

In one night, Arlo had gotten everything he'd ever wanted.

He glanced over at Dimitri, whose eyes focused on the dark ahead. "I love you."

The car swerved as Dimitri darted his gaze towards him. "What?"

"I think I always have," Arlo said, nodding his head as if that would somehow make Dimitri believe him.

"Why are you saying this?" Dimitri asked, frowning.

Arlo smiled softly. "Because I don't know if I'll have the chance to say it when we get there and I've wanted to say it every day since you walked back into my life, so I thought now was as good a time as ever, before we walk into the unknown. I just wanted you to know."

Dimitri's grip on the steering wheel tightened until he was white-knuckled. "I'm not saying it back," he snapped.

Arlo felt like somebody had slammed his heart in the car door. "Okay," he said, voice thick.

He wasn't sure why he'd expected anything different. He'd hoped for one last moment to cling to, but some part of him had known Dimitri saying those words back was a bridge too far.

Dimitri suddenly swerved across three lanes of traffic, ripping a gasp from Arlo as he skidded to a halt.

Dimitri threw the car into park, turning to look at him. "Don't do this."

Arlo shook his head. "Do what?" he asked.

Dimitri's nostrils flared, his jaw muscle ticking. "Don't give me some grand finale speech like we're about to Thelma and Louise ourselves over a cliff. I can fix this. I can. Everything's going to be fine."

"But if it isn't—" Arlo started.

Dimitri's hands gripped Arlo's sweatshirt, pulling him

close until their foreheads touched. "No. You don't get to give me some weepy I love you. Because that sounds a lot like goodbye and I'm not letting you go." He started kissing Arlo's lips over and over. "I'm not letting you go," he soothed. "I won't."

Tears streamed down Arlo's cheeks as he clung to Dimitri, too. "I know you think you can fix this, but somebody knows what we did. We're fucked. *I'm* fucked. I don't want to go my whole life without telling you how I feel."

Dimitri shook his head like he was rejecting Arlo's words. "I'm not going anywhere. Neither of us are. If I have to kill someone tonight to make this all go away, I will. If I have to kill a dozen people to protect you, I will. I need you to understand that. I will never let another bad thing happen to you. I just won't."

"You can't kill everybody," Arlo wailed.

"I can try. That's the beauty of somebody like me. I don't feel regret. I don't feel guilt or anger or remorse. If somebody tries to get between us, I will kill them and I won't shed a single tear." He took Arlo's face in his hands. "I was born to protect you."

Arlo's heart was exploding with joy and pain. He'd wanted to hear this for so long, but he didn't want to hear it like this, when they were both desperate and scared. "I want to protect you, too. I want to keep you safe, too. You're the only person in my life who has ever cared if I lived or died. I can't lose you."

"You won't. Please. Just don't give up on us yet," Dimitri begged. "Please."

Arlo couldn't bring himself to lie, so he just clung to him, fat tears rolling down his face to drip between them. There was no way out of this.

When Arlo's tears dried, he released Dimitri, sniffling. "We should probably go. Whoever sent that note is waiting on us."

Dimitri gave a single nod, shifting the car into drive before easing back onto the road. Five miles later, they exited the empty interstate to a somehow even emptier highway.

It was impossibly dark. There wasn't a gas station or even a truck stop, just a long open stretch of pavement. They drove, using the GPS to navigate, as there were no discernible landmarks to help them differentiate one dark dirt road from another. They didn't have street signs. Dimitri called them access roads.

Finally, the GPS led them onto a barely-there dirt road, ending at an open chain-link fence. Past that, the terrain became rough, the narrow path that led them deeper onto the property made of little more than broken chunks of asphalt. The place had a distinct smell to it. Like gasoline and burned rubber. It might have had something to do with the precariously stacked cars lining either side of the drive.

"What the hell is this place?" Arlo whispered, feeling like, if he spoke too loud, he might wake whatever monster lurked among the ruins.

"It's a salvage yard," Dimitri confirmed. "They buy junk cars and scrap them for parts."

Perspiration broke out along Arlo's hairline. Nobody

would ever find them out there. Their GPS led to someplace entirely different. Could Calliope see where they really were, even if she was spoofing their GPS? Did she know they hadn't listened to her? That they'd taken off into the night to follow instructions some pregnant stranger had scrawled on white paper with a thick black sharpie?

Dimitri turned off the car, taking a deep breath. "No matter what happens, you stay close."

"Yeah, that won't be a problem," Arlo promised, staring at the entrance of what looked like a metallic maze.

Outside the car, Arlo wrapped himself around Dimitri's arm, letting him drag him deeper into the yard. The silence was deafening. Arlo forced himself to concentrate on his own breathing just to keep his ears from ringing.

They approached a small building in the center of the facility, but when they tried the door, it was locked tight. Dimitri steered him around the side where they found another open gate separating the front from the back, stopping short in a clearing of sorts to stare upwards at an enormous piece of machinery.

"What in the actual fuck is that?" Arlo whispered.

"I have no idea," Dimitri said.

There was a sound like an electrical current tripping and then bulbs flared to life above, leaving them standing in a wide spotlight. They both covered their eyes, blinking, as a figure walked out of the darkness. "It's a car crusher."

Arlo gripped Dimitri tighter as he squinted, waiting for the man's features to become clearer. He wore all black, right down to the leather gloves covering his hands. Arlo knew him. They both did. He was a Mulvaney.

"August, right?" Dimitri asked.

The man gave a cool smile. "Yes. I apologize for all the cloak and dagger stuff with my assistant, Cricket, but I thought it might be good practice should this be the beginning of your life of crime and not the end. Besides, I wasn't certain you were trustworthy."

"Trustworthy?" Dimitri echoed.

"Mm, people do dumb things when they're cornered. And while I trust your mother implicitly, I don't know you. But you clearly know of us, which was not only a surprise but a liability."

Arlo didn't know the Mulvaney family. They were just a name in the paper, sometimes a picture on the cover of a tabloid. It was clear after tonight; they were much more than that. But it had never occurred to Arlo to tell the world what he knew. What did he know, in the grand scheme of things?

"To be fair, my mother didn't tell me about you. I figured it out myself," Dimitri said. "It took a long time for me to put the pieces together, but the truth is, I never really cared enough to look that hard. Your family is none of my business."

Was that why this man had brought them there to the salvage yard? To tie up loose ends? Had they just delivered themselves on a silver platter to a murderer?

"Are you going to kill us?" Arlo heard himself blurt.

August somewhat assuaged his fears when he gave a surprised chuckle. "Is that what you think? That I've brought you out here to the middle of nowhere to get rid of you?"

"It seems a valid fear," Arlo countered, looking once more at the machine rising behind him.

"I suppose that's fair. But no. You have nothing to fear from me." He looked at Dimitri. "I'm the one who should be afraid. I've directly disobeyed your mother."

Dimitri frowned. "What do you mean?"

"She asked that we stay out of it. My guess is that she wants you to clean up your own mess. A little life lesson on why murder is never the answer. And while I respect her thought process, she's wrong."

"Wrong?" Arlo muttered, his pulse pounding in his throat and his tongue glued to the roof of his mouth.

"Yes. Wrong. You can't unring a bell, and you can't simply know how to cover your tracks if nobody's given you the skills or tools to do so. So, allow me to give you your first lesson. No body, no crime."

Arlo's heart thudded heavily against his ribs, his tongue glued to the roof of his mouth as the man paced before them like he was giving a lecture to a new batch of students.

"What does that mean?" Dimitri asked.

August's smile chilled Arlo to his core. "It means Holden no longer has a corporeal form."

"You burned him?" Arlo asked.

"Burning leaves behind bones, teeth. Your abusive ex-boyfriend is nothing but a memory."

"Why?" Dimitri asked. "Why would you help us?"

August shrugged. "The reason my family is so good at what we do is that we don't kill people on impulse. By the time we pull the trigger—metaphorically speaking—our alibis are already in place and we know whether it's better to make the victim disappear or to stage the crime scene."

Arlo shivered at his matter-of-fact tone. "Okay."

"But when you kill impulsively, you're left to…split the baby, so to speak. Calliope was forced to decide whether she would help you create an alibi or focus on damage control."

"Damage control meaning what?" Dimitri asked.

"When people go missing, families worry. They make phone calls, they call the police."

"Are you saying people are looking for Holden?" Arlo asked, panic climbing into his voice. "Did his dad call the cops? Are they looking at us?"

August raised his hand as if to silence Arlo. "I've taken care of it."

"You, what?" Dimitri asked.

August sighed. "I'm sure Calliope did what was best in the moment, but this was far too big for you to handle yourselves. And I say that selfishly. Exposing you could expose all of us. My family can't have that."

"What does that mean? What did you do?"

"Holden doesn't exist anymore," August said ominously, glancing behind him at the car crusher. "And neither does his car."

Arlo shook his head. "But…his father won't just let it go. He's rich. Connected."

August waved a hand. "Oh, I'm aware. I did my research. The thing is, with people like corrupt federal judges, you have to make them think they're the ones getting away

with murder."

"Meaning…" Arlo asked, breathless.

"Meaning the judge received a series of increasingly frantic texts from Holden explaining that he'd done something terrible and had to get out of the country. Now."

"And his father just bought that?" Dimitri asked.

August shrugged. "Probably not at first, but there was an accompanying name and date in the texts that, when investigated, would point to a monstrous crime that was well within someone like Holden's temperament. This puts the judge in the position of making a very dangerous choice. If he suspects Holden's not the one texting him and alerts the police, he risks putting his son on the radar for the aforementioned crime. Conversely, he can just take his son at face value and tell him to get the hell out of the country. Which is what he did."

"And you think that's enough?" Arlo asked.

"Honestly?" August said with a smile. "I think it's overkill. According to Calliope, he was in the closet, so there was no real tie between the two of you. No reason to think that you would somehow have any involvement with the man's disappearance. Sure, they might have seen your split lip and thought Holden was a gay-bashing douchebag, but I don't think they would have fingered you as someone capable of caving his skull in."

"But I did," Arlo muttered.

"Oh, I know. It's impressive, really."

"Thanks?" Arlo said. "So, what do we do now?"

"Nothing. You do nothing. You go home, and you live

your lives and you forget this night ever happened. The judge won't file a missing person's report. He'll likely make sure people everywhere know that Holden's studying abroad or taking a mental health break."

"But eventually, the judge will figure out Holden's not where he thinks he is," Dimitri said.

"And by then, it will be far too late for him to do anything about it. Any evidence behind the coffee shop will have washed away. Holden's car is a cube of scrap metal and, without his body, there's no proof a crime even took place."

Arlo shook his head. "That can't be it. We just go on with our lives?"

August shrugged. "You know all our secrets. I suppose you could train to work with us like the others, but you're quite young. Maybe just go back to school and finish your education."

With that, August turned and walked away, but then stopped short. "Oh, and apologize to your mother for me. She scares me a little."

For a long while, Dimitri and Arlo just stood there in the cold before returning to the car without saying a word. Once inside, Arlo turned to look at Dimitri. "So, that's it? We just got away with murder?"

Dimitri leaned in close. "I think so, yeah."

Arlo just blinked at Dimitri. "I don't know if I'm relieved or numb."

"I love you, too," Dimitri said, grabbing Arlo's face in his hands.

"What?" Arlo asked, bewildered.

"I said I wouldn't say it like that, like it was the end for us. But I can say it now. Now that it's just the beginning. "

"So say it," Arlo said, breathless. "Say it again."

Dimitri grinned, kissing him deeply. "I love you. I have loved you my whole life. I will keep loving you for the rest of it."

Arlo flung his arms around Dimitri's neck, burying his face there. "I love you, too." They held each other for a long moment, then Arlo said, "Do you think we should call your mom and tell her we're alive?"

Dimitri nodded. "Yeah. Probably."

"She's going to be pissed," Arlo said.

"Very."

"She's probably going to yell a lot."

Dimitri sighed, voice resigned. "Most likely."

"Maybe we call her when we get home, instead?" Arlo suggested, pulling back to give him a hopeful look.

Dimitri grinned, smacking a kiss on Arlo's lips. "Yeah, maybe we do that."

Arlo leaned in for a longer kiss. "And maybe we stop and get food at that twenty-four-hour diner that we passed a few exits back? I'm starving."

Arlo's stomach dipped as Dimitri dropped a kiss to Arlo's forehead, "Whatever you want, babe."

"So the babe thing is here to stay?" Arlo teased.

"What? You don't like babe?"

Arlo wrinkled his nose, shaking his head. "It's a little generic." When Dimitri protested, Arlo held up a hand. "You know what, we'll workshop it over pancakes."

EPILOGUE
DIMITRI

"You're in Mr. Daniels' *Intro to Anatomy* **class, right?"**

Before Dimitri could answer, Arlo bent down to liberate the cup lids from beneath the counter, snagging his attention away from the blonde-haired girl. Arlo could have squatted down like he usually did, but this was his less-than-subtle way of reminding Dimitri why there was nothing on the other side of that counter better than what he already had.

Dimitri didn't need the reminder, but he sure as hell appreciated the way Arlo's khakis hugged his oh-so-perfect ass.

"That'll be three fifty," Dimitri told the girl, distracted, his gaze still glued to Arlo.

"I—"

Jason hopped up on the counter directly in front of the girl. "You must be new around here, sweetheart, 'cause my man here is strictly dickly."

"What?" the girl said, startled.

"Yeah, he's gay, girl. That little dainty thing with his ass in the air? That's his boyfriend. He looks cute and adorable, but if you look at his man for too long, he's gonna come at you like a spider monkey." Dimitri snickered, but Arlo flicked Jason off without looking. Jason was undeterred. He swung his ball cap backwards, leaning in close. "I, on the other hand, am one hundred percent straight."

Dimitri snorted. "Liar."

Jason looked at him, wounded. "What happens during rush week stays at rush week, damn." He turned back to the girl, who now looked somewhere between confused and amused. "That still makes me ninety-seven percent straight, at least. Besides, a modern woman like yourself probably wants somebody…open-minded?"

The girl rolled her eyes but handed her phone to Jason so he could put his information in before they both retreated to the corner booth where Jason was holding court with Mandy and the others.

Mandy had calmed down a lot. She was actually far more tolerable since Arlo had put her in her place. She hardly ever brought up her short-lived movie career and, if pressed, she would tell everybody that she and Arlo were great friends. Arlo would not agree, but nobody ever asked him.

Before Dimitri could signal to the next customer that he was ready for them, Arlo scooted up behind him, his hands covertly roaming as he rose on his tiptoes to press his lips to Dimitri's ear.

"If you keep getting distracted by me, Maggie won't let us work together anymore, remember?" he crooned.

Dimitri remembered. Maggie had taken them both into

her office just two days ago to, yet again, tell them to save the 'grab-ass'—her words—for when they were at home.

Home.

It still didn't feel real that Dimitri got to go to bed with Arlo every night and wake up with him in the morning. They even had a pet, sort of. An ugly as fuck rat named Scabbers.

Who chose a rat as a pet?

Arlo. He'd found it in the back, in one of Maggie's traps. It had closed on the rat's tail, sending Arlo into a crying fit until Dimitri had agreed to take it to the vet and then to rehab it. That rehab had turned into a cage and a name and Dimitri coming home to Arlo cuddling a kitten-sized rat most nights. If that wasn't love, Dimitri didn't know what was.

Dimitri supposed he could have said no. But, honestly, he didn't want to. If Arlo had asked for a kidney, Dimitri would ask which one he wanted. And that was just facts.

He reached behind him, wrapping his hands around Arlo, squeezing his ass briefly before letting his hands fall.

"Tease," Arlo whispered.

"You started it," Dimitri said under his breath.

"And, as soon as that sign flips closed, I'm going to finish it, too," Arlo assured him, pinching his ass before walking away.

Six months had passed since Holden's untimely demise, and August Mulvaney had been right. Nobody gave a fuck that Holden had disappeared. Dimitri's mother still kept tabs on the chatter, just in case. In the beginning, she would feed the rumor mill. But now, it ran all on its own. People at Holden's school all had theories, ranging from him having fled the country with his father's money to a serial killer having murdered him. He was becoming an urban legend. That one had been a little too close for comfort.

Arlo was a whole new person without Holden around. He was flirty, confident; he smiled all the time. It hadn't happened overnight. The first month, he'd been a wreck, having panic attacks almost nightly, nightmares where they carted him off to prison or where Holden had come back from the dead to exact his revenge.

Then he'd agreed to therapy. Luckily, the campus offered it to students for free as part of their mental health initiative. And though Arlo couldn't go in there and talk about the time he murdered his abusive ex-boyfriend, he could work through a lot of his family shit. He still had no contact with them, but, truthfully, that was the healthiest option in Dimitri's opinion.

Besides, Arlo had Calliope. Dimitri's mother had swooped in and adopted him almost immediately. It was a good thing Dimitri lacked the normal range of emotions or it might have hurt his feelings how much his mother preferred Arlo over him. She baked him cookies, called him on the phone a couple of times a week. They texted each other almost daily. Sometimes, they even combined forces to conspire against him. Arlo called her Mom.

And Dimitri loved it. He loved Arlo's newfound confidence, loved going to bed with him at night and waking up to him in the morning. Arlo still needed a lot of attention. There were a lot of wounds that hadn't healed, not physically but emotionally. Sometimes, he was still afraid to initiate sex for fear of being rejected. Other times, he wanted Dimitri to tell him all the things he loved about him.

It wasn't a hardship. Dimitri had been collecting things to love about Arlo since before they could do basic math, and he'd never refused a chance to show Arlo just how much he wanted him. And he did. He couldn't get enough. Sinking into Arlo's body was the closest thing to home Dimitri had ever experienced. He'd never felt as needed or wanted as when Arlo was begging for more.

Dimitri shook the thought away before he got a very inappropriate work boner. There was only another twenty minutes before they closed, and then Arlo was all his. He finished ringing up the next customer, then started the close out work. Arlo kept throwing smug little smirks at Dimitri as he knocked items off their list at double time.

The moment Dimitri locked the door and flipped the sign to closed, he turned on Arlo, who flicked his gaze to the camera trained on them, slowly backing away until he was safely out from under its watchful eye. Dimitri swallowed hard as Arlo slipped off his apron and went for his belt buckle.

"You are such a fucking tease," Dimitri growled again.

"Who's teasing?" Arlo taunted, crooking his finger, beckoning him closer.

Dimitri hopped the counter without warning, catching Arlo before he could run, trapping him against the wall of the short hallway. Arlo's pupils blew wide as Dimitri held him against the wall by his neck. He didn't apply any pressure, just held him in place so he could slant their mouths together in a dirty kiss.

He used his free hand to release Arlo's already straining cock, working him with firm strokes. "Right here?" Arlo asked between kisses, already bucking up into his fist.

Dimitri bit at his lips. "Unless you really do want me to fuck you on Maggie's desk. Is that what you want?" he rumbled. "You know how much I love bending you over, and I haven't been inside you all day."

Arlo moaned into his mouth, his hips moving faster, but he shook his head. "No. The last time we did that, you improvised with the lube situation and I almost ended up in the hospital."

Dimitri dipped his tongue into Arlo's mouth. "Vanilla syrup seemed like a viable option. I was already down there having my dessert. How was I supposed to know it would cause friction?"

"Basic physics?" Arlo teased, freeing Dimitri's cock, shoving his jeans and underwear to mid-thigh, making an appreciative noise when he saw he was hard. "Fuck, I love your dick."

"It loves you, too," Dimitri assured him. "What do you want, baby?"

Arlo wrapped his arms around Dimitri's neck and jumped, his legs closing around his hips. "Quick and dirty. You can fuck me when we get home. Right now, I just want to get off. Make me come."

"So bossy," Dimitri muttered, gripping Arlo's ass until

their cocks slotted together and they both groaned. "This what you want?"

Arlo pulled back and glanced over Dimitri's shoulder. "No."

Dimitri frowned, confused. "No?"

Arlo leaned back, bracing himself against the wall before planting his feet on the opposite wall behind Dimitri. Arlo ran his tongue over his palm before taking them both in his spit-slick grip.

"You really are a spider-monkey," Dimitri managed, sparks of electricity shooting off behind his eyelids at the feel of Arlo's hand on him. "Fuck, that feels good. Keep going."

Arlo picked up the pace, his strokes practiced and sure. He knew every trick to get Dimitri off, and yet, it never got boring, mostly because what got Dimitri off was watching Arlo get off.

When he threw his head back, tiny little cries falling from his lips, Dimitri batted his hand away, taking over so Arlo could just feel.

"Yes, God. Keep doing that. Do the thing with your thumb," Arlo panted. Dimitri smiled, sweeping his thumb across his slit, cock throbbing as Arlo moaned like a porn star, his lids at half-mast. "Yeah, do it again. Fuck, I'm already so close. I've wanted this all day, needed your hands on me all fucking day."

Heat gathered at the base of Dimitri's spine, as much from Arlo's stream of conscious ramblings as from the feel of his fist working over them both. "You don't have to wait for me. You know what watching you get off does to me. Show me."

Arlo's teeth clamped down on his bottom lip, stifling another low moan as he rolled his hips upward into Dimitri's fist. "Oh, fuck. Oh, fuck."

Dimitri watched as Arlo spilled over his fist, working him until he cried out. Dimitri gathered his cum, smearing it over his cock, before jerking himself with intention, just wanting to get off.

This time, it was Arlo who batted Dimitri's hand away, wrapping his fist around him and working him with sticky fingers, his gaze glued to Dimitri's, still watching for any sign he was doing something wrong.

Dimitri tried to assure him he wasn't. He pressed his forehead to his, panting out, "That's it, baby. You feel so good. That feels so good. I'm gonna come."

As his orgasm hit him, he gripped Arlo's hip tighter, his brain shutting down any higher thought process other than *fuck, yes,* his knees feeling a little like Jell-O.

When he opened his eyes, Arlo was still leaning back against the wall, looking up at him from beneath thick dark lashes, his cum-coated fingers now in his mouth.

Dimitri's gaze locked onto Arlo's perfect mouth and his cum glistening on his lips. "Yeah, you're definitely getting fucked when we get home."

Arlo dropped his feet from the wall, and they spent a few minutes awkwardly righting their clothing.

"What do we tell Maggie to explain that?" Arlo asked casually.

Dimitri turned to glance behind him, a bark of laughter escaping as he saw Arlo's perfect boot prints a quarter of the way up the wall. "That's your problem. You're opening with her tomorrow."

Arlo shook his head. "Uh-uh. I'm gonna call out sick."

Dimitri picked Arlo up, tossing him over his shoulder. "You're only delaying the inevitable. Besides, it's not like she's actually going to fire either of us. Nobody else wants to work here."

"I'll just blame you," Arlo said, slapping Dimitri's ass.

Dimitri swatted his ass back a little harder. "What was that?"

"I'll blame you," Arlo said louder, as if Dimitri were hard of hearing.

Six months ago, Arlo would have panicked over being questioned, over Dimitri's casual swat on the butt. But there was trust there. Trust that Dimitri had earned.

Arlo snagged their bags as they walked past the bench. "Put me down."

"Nope," Dimitri said, swinging the back door open to the warm night air.

The heavy door slammed shut behind him, and he stopped short. A tall man leaned against Dimitri's Toyota, arms crossed over his chest. Even obscured by shadow, he looked familiar.

As he moved closer, he realized he knew him. Another Mulvaney. One of the twins. And he wasn't alone. There was a thinner man beside him, with blond hair and large wire-rimmed glasses that shouldn't have looked good on anybody but looked right at home on him.

"What's wrong? What's happening? Why did you stop?" Arlo asked. "I'm getting dizzy."

Dimitri carefully set Arlo on his feet before turning him to see their guests. Arlo gasped, backing directly into Dimitri, who put an arm around his chest to steady him.

"What are you doing here?" Dimitri asked.

"We need a favor," the twin said.

Dimitri squinted. "Which one are you?"

The man moved forward until he was no longer in the shadows. "Asa. This is Zane. We need your help."

"What kind of help?" Dimitri asked.

"Does it matter?" Asa countered, the question weighted.

Dimitri gave a heavy sigh. No. No, it didn't. When somebody's family helped you get rid of a body, that family had the right to ask for favors. "Have you cleared this with my mom? I really can't afford to get on her bitch list again."

Asa's responding grin was unsettling. "My dad cleared it with your mom. All parental units are in the loop. Let's go get some food. I'm starving."

Arlo glanced over his shoulder at Dimitri. "Are we really doing this?"

"What choice do we have?" Dimitri shrugged.

Asa nodded. "Exactly. Glad we're all on the same page. We'll take my car. It's right over there."

As they watched, Asa snaked an arm around the waist of the other man, Zane, who didn't look thrilled about the gesture, but he didn't protest either.

"What do you think their deal is?" Arlo asked.

"I think it's none of our business," Dimitri whispered, lacing their fingers together.

"So much for getting fucked tonight," Arlo said, forlorn.

Dimitri tugged Arlo up under his arm, their fingers still intertwined. "Oh, we might still get fucked tonight, but not in the way either of us was hoping."

"Christ, you two are giving me a toothache with all the cuteness," Asa crowed from ten paces ahead.

"Then go kidnap two other people," Arlo quipped.

Dimitri grinned at Arlo's bravado. He'd definitely come a long way.

"Oh, don't tempt him. He loves holding people against their will," his companion grumbled.

"Don't be sassy, Lois Lane," Asa said, dropping his hand to the other man's ass. "They might think you don't like me."

Zane wiggled out of Asa's grip. "I don't like you."

Asa scoffed. "The scratches down my back say otherwise, sugar britches."

"Gross," Arlo groaned, earning a laugh from Asa.

He gestured to the backseat of a large black SUV. "Chop-chop, young lovers. There's fuckery afoot."

The Mulvaneys were a strange fucking lot, and the twins seemed the weirdest of the bunch. It was odd seeing them away from each other. Even in pictures, he'd never seen the two photographed apart. It was weird. Like seeing a teacher at a strip club or a dog walk on its hind legs. Asa and Avi Mulvaney were never separated. Except, now, they were.

The two of them climbed up into the bench seat, squeezing together in the center. Up front, Asa buckled

Zane's seatbelt, then glanced at them in the rearview mirror. "Jesus, relax, you two. I just need some information. I'm not here to rip off your toenails with pliers."

"Well, that adds a whole new layer of horror to this," Arlo muttered.

"Don't worry, baby. I will keep your toenails safely where they belong," Dimitri promised.

"That is both gross and romantic," Arlo said, a smile spreading across his face.

"That's me. Grossly romantic." Dimitri leaned down to drop a kiss on his forehead. "And for the record, there's nobody else I'd rather be kidnapped with."

Arlo looked up at him with soft eyes. "Aw, me neither. I love you."

"I love you, too," Dimitri crooned.

"And I love noise canceling headphones," Zane said around a groan, glaring at Asa. "Can you put some music on or something?"

Asa winked at him. "Anything for you, darling."

Zane sighed in exasperation, but Dimitri grinned. There really wasn't anybody else in the world Dimitri would rather be kidnapped with, and that really was as close to love as a psychopath like him would ever get.

ABOUT THE AUTHOR

ONLEY JAMES is the pen name of YA author, Martina McAtee, who lives in Central Florida with her children, her pitbull, her weiner dog, and an ever-growing collection of shady looking cats. She splits her time between writing YA LGBT paranormal romances and writing adult m/m romances.

When not at her desk, you can find her mainlining Starbucks refreshers, whining about how much she has to do, and avoiding the things she has to do by binge-watching unhealthy amounts of television in one sitting. She loves ghost stories, true crime documentaries, obsessively scrolling social media, and writing kinky, snarky books about men who fall in love with other men.

Find her online at:
WWW.ONLEYJAMES.COM